PEDRO THE VAST

A NOVEL

Simón López Trujillo

Translated by Robin Myers

ALGONQUIN BOOKS OF CHAPEL HILL

LITTLE, BROWN AND COMPANY

Copyright © 2021 by Simón López Trujillo
Translation Copyright © 2026 by Robin Myers

Algonquin Books of Chapel Hill / Little, Brown and Company
Hachette Book Group
1290 Avenue of the Americas, New York, NY 10104
littlebrown.com

First published as *El vasto territorio* by Alfaguara in 2021, in Chile
First English Language Edition: January 2026

Algonquin Books of Chapel Hill is an imprint of Little, Brown and Company, a division of Hachette Book Group, Inc. The Algonquin Books name and logo are trademarks of Hachette Book Group, Inc.

The publisher is not responsible for websites (or their content) that are not owned by the publisher.

The Hachette Speakers Bureau provides a wide range of authors for speaking events. To find out more, go to hachettespeakersbureau.com or email hachettespeakers@hbgusa.com.

Little, Brown and Company books may be purchased in bulk for business, educational, or promotional use. For information, please contact your local bookseller or the Hachette Book Group Special Markets Department at special.markets@hbgusa.com.

Illustration on page 48 © Baltazar Pérez; all other illustrations courtesy of Kidd, S. E., F. Hagen, R. L. Tscharke, M. Huynh, K. H. Bartlett, M. Fyfe, L. MacDougall, T. Boekhout, K. J. Kwon-Chung, and W. Meyer. 2004. "A Rare Genotype of Cryptococcus Gattii Caused the Cryptococcosis Outbreak on Vancouver Island (British Columbia, Canada)." *Proceedings of the National Academy of Sciences* 101 (49): 17258–63. HYPERLINK "https://url.us.m.mimecastprotect.com/s/ZsvwCgJDQJCkY01Ds NfNf4xAhv?domain=doi.org"https://doi.org/10.1073/pnas.0402981101.

ISBN 9781643757100
Library of Congress Control Number: 2025940258

Printing 1, 2025

LSC-C

Printed in the United States of America

PEDRO
THE
VAST

I remember walking under the great eucalyptus in the park,
when the field was covered in dense clouds.
In the silence and in that kind of happy blindness, I heard
the towering noise of the leaves and trunk of the
    tremendous tree.
And then there was no difference among earth or sky
or human beings.

José María Arguedas, *El Sexto*

Thought is an attribute of God.

Baruch Spinoza, *Ethics*
translated by H. R. M. Elwes

PEDRO
THE
VAST

PART ONE

THE DREAM OF THE EUCALYPTUS CHILDREN

I'd say I opened my eyes, but I'm not sure. I wouldn't say I awoke. Looking back on it, the dream felt like climbing into a kettle. Awaiting the boil, swirling, faint, in bubbles that struggled toward the noise. It was all of us together. I opened my eyes and saw, of course, but nothing looked the same. Lord knows if there are other verbs for such matters.

A clearing in the woods. The perspective was as if shot from below. Like if someone had buried a pair of eyes, watering them carefully, in steady sun, until the eyelids papering the seed had let themselves split open to reveal the baby creature, always seeking the sky through the curtain of a playhouse. If that's what looking is—you know? I'm not sure what I saw, but I saw so much. Way up high and all the way along, I saw the meadow being the meadow, the woods, the woods, but the moss inside told me things, and I knew I couldn't repeat any part of what I'd heard. I only listened and that was what it was. Suddenly all things sprouted all together like the water rising, turning to steam.

Leaves, lichen, shoots, stone, water, lots of water, a little semen, yes, dead slithering things, residues of beast, gasoline, almost snowy with fungus; a bit of fire was also there, but it went out. A strong wind blew, the wind always bearing things far away, doing things. It wasn't the fire, you know; the part at the beginning was only the wind that returned and spoke to itself.

Like I said, lots of water, but lots of plants, I also saw. They weren't green: The plants beneath weren't the same plants, they said things in a better language, they spoke among themselves out of nervousness, they knew what each wanted to ask before doing so, it didn't take much thought. The wind soothed everything, brought rain, allowed for wetness, and that was a pleasure. I remember we bathed in it, yes, as I remember other ancient things. The fragrance of flowers someone left on the kitchen table in my childhood home. But that wasn't a house, I don't think, it's more of a well we're talking about. Yes, that I do remember, the water above. Not beneath. In the earth we were all of us and not a word, not a blink to anyone of what I saw. If I speak now, it's not because they've asked me to. It's because of my son. He and I were mute. Dry plants for a long time. But not anymore.

THE CHAINSAWS WENT quiet all at once. Pedro lowered his arms and rested his machine against a tree. He took off his helmet and wiped the sweat from the visor. Daylight savings meant an earlier dusk, but he still left work at the same time: His departure was as dark as his arrival in the morning. He collected his things and went to change with the rest of the crew.

He imagined the heat of an invisible cigarette as the truck swayed along. Half an hour for a Sudoku sheet, not speaking to anyone. Patricio, his son, had given him a book of those mysterious puzzles. He found them so strange at first. It's simple actually, Pato had said. You just have to find the right number. Now, with patient practice, he'd made it halfway through the book. He'd just started the hard level and was struggling not to fall asleep before he finished the first exercise. He held the sheet against the back of a snoring coworker and his pencil trembled, at the mercy of the dirt road.

Toward the end of the ride, he decided to get out a little early and pick up something to eat for later. He felt in his pocket for the necklace of eucalyptus pods he'd made. They were like gleaming gems, the little cones coated in green moss. Secret emeralds he treasured between his fingertips. Before, he used to give them to Pato for his collection, but his son was too old for that now, so he made chokers for Catalina. In the chill of the night, his breathing was punctuated by a deep, heavy cough, like a dog's. Dejected and weary, clutching a bag of bread, Pedro walked with a fist pressed to his mouth.

As he opened the door, Cata dropped the pencil she used for her homework and threw her arms around him. Pedro hugged her and went to the kitchen, took out a pot, filled it with water, added some long dry leaves he'd extracted from a jar in the cabinet. He covered the pot with a cloth, lit the burner, and sat to wait for everything to boil.

"Are you making that weird mixture again?"

"It's just eucalyptus steam. An expectorant. Good for a cough."

"I know. Can I help?"

"No, it's okay. Go give your sister a hand."

Pedro lifted the cloth when the water reached a boil and the kitchen filled with fragrant vapor. Cata asked when they were going to eat. Pato told her to focus on the assignment, said a quotient meant how many times something is contained in another thing, stop resting her chin in her hands and hold the pencil properly.

Pedro shut his eyes, letting the steam sear his face. He took a long, deep breath until he felt his lungs open like the doors of a train and a sense of elation lifted him up, an eagerness that reminded him of the time he and María traveled up north, their plans to get married, the colors they glimpsed through the window of that train from Concepción to La Calera, seven thirty in the morning, sitting together in the second car, the soothing smell, then the heat seeping into his nostrils, expelling phlegm that had been caught in his throat for weeks, like the wheels of a stopped machine starting to whir. A violent cough, then the watery emerald Pedro spat into the sink.

Once Catalina was asleep, Pedro tossed his backpack, reeking of the day's clothes, into the bedroom. As he tugged off his boots, he felt a strange presence in his hand, spreading over his skin like damp hair. He swore under his breath and wiped the moss on his pants, his arms, the chest of the thin pajama shirt he'd worn for years. The sticky organism reminded him of the next day's labors and the scent of the forest. He got into bed. In a single deft gesture, the sheets drew his body from the light. He closed his eyes and coughed again.

Outside, the neighborhood dogs barked at a pale, still moon whose light revealed certain objects: the pair of boots at the foot of the bed, clothes tossed onto a chair, a nightstand crowded with family photos and a darkened portrait, half the TV set, three ends of a cross nailed into the iron headboard, reflections in the glass over an autographed Fernández Vial shirt, framed and hung on the wall, various cosmetics and creams all coated in a fine layer of dust that looked like dew in the half-light.

Curanilahue hadn't been like this until recently. The water wasn't always that color. Why doesn't Catalina want to do her homework. When are parent-teacher conferences. What happened today to that bastard Juan Carlos. What's the deal with this fucking cough. María was right: The city had gotten so sad. What's the math teacher's name. So poor. They should leave. Probably Tuesday. The river used to be beautiful. The cool water. She was so pretty. The rain-slicked tracks and the Spanish moss hanging from the hawthorns. My dad happy to hear I was getting married. Pamela? In her beekeeping suit. Her spring dress. Mariana? The pots of honey in the yard. The clear water where the bees went to drink. The estuary swelling enormous. A floating house.

⚙

GIOVANNA JOLTED AWAKE. It was still dark and the alarm hadn't gone off yet. She let out a deep sigh, pulling the quilt up to her shoulders and curling into a fetal position. In fifteen more minutes, her cell phone would show the first signs of morning on the nightstand, the noise, the daily riff that would continue in later conversations, the neighbors' poodle barking, thumps on the shower knob, text messages, drills, jib cranes, steamrollers and shouting from the nearby construction site, dirty plates, traffic, a thousand loudspeakers, clumsy coworkers, the hum of people in the street, talking on the phone, arguing in a restaurant, laughing and crying at the same time, the genomic sequence, the stained lab coat in the laundry, the idiotic neighbor lady and her fights with her husband, the stuck knob in the shower, the hot water that won't come, that runs out quickly, cut off, like the melody of a flute that clatters to the floor.

Giovanna had fallen back asleep. The fifteen minutes dilated there, snagged between dark trees. She was running far into the distance. She felt chased by fire, fleeing through the woods, afraid she'd stumble.

Two hours later, she parked outside the lab and waited before getting out of the car. She took a long, hard breath, eyes shut, as if trying to use up all her air, expel it from her body.

Entering the lab, she greeted her coworkers with a swift rearrangement of her face. She felt uneasy. She went to her spot, set her phone on the desk, pulled back her hair, draped her jacket over the seat, put on her white coat, opened a fridge, and removed the petri dishes she'd put there the day before. She placed them on the table and examined each one under the microscope, jotting down data in a notebook. She spent the entire morning this way.

As she watched the coffee machine burble and fill, she tried to calculate how many panic attacks she'd had in her life. She remembered an afternoon when she hadn't been able to find her running shoes. The sun was bright outside and she'd gone two days without leaving the apartment, working on a series of calculations for her dissertation. It was her third year studying mycology at the University of Manchester. She'd just finished the genomic sequence for a lichen and set up a calculation on her lab computer that would process remotely, and she decided to go for a run, take advantage of the weather. She put on an athletic hoodie, leggings, and clean socks, but she couldn't find her sneakers. They weren't under the table or the couch or hidden under the books, magazines, and mugs scattered all over the living room, bedroom, terrace, and kitchen. She sat down on the bed, wondered how it was possible. They had to be somewhere. The only person who'd come by in recent days was Tiffany, who'd slept over on Sunday night. But there was no way. She couldn't have taken them.

Then she noticed a small spot on her chest that was sucking the air inward, a pressure in her arms that made them go limp. She placed her hands on the wall, curved over herself. She couldn't speak or move. She stayed still, scarcely feeling the air that passed in and out of her. It was like standing in the sleet. A white, paralyzing cold that gripped her in broad daylight in the English spring.

Some afternoons, alone in the lab, something returned her to that moment. She'd learned to face it over time. She'd rest her hands on the metal counter. She'd stay completely emotionless, letting herself sink. Close her eyes. Count through the series of prime numbers.

·❂·

THE MEDIAN STRIP was wet and the sun was slow to heat it. Patricio walked home after taking his sister to school, hands stuffed into his pockets. Beside him, a highway with occasional passing cars, so few that there was no sense in counting them. A dog was sprawled in one lane. Its body caught the sun like a circus floodlight. For a moment, it met Patricio's eyes, and he thought with tenderness and longing of his dead dog Celerino.

He opened the front gate and entered the house. No one else was home. He went to his room, got his laptop, and brought it to the living room table. He pushed aside his sister's math book, turned on the computer, and clicked on a porn site. He unzipped his jeans and lowered them a bit, baring himself to the top of his thighs, and poised his bare buttocks on the cloth of the chair.

Halfway through the video, a girl in his grade sent him a Facebook message. How was he doing, she asked. With a rush of anxiety and awkwardness, he lifted his left hand to the keyboard. He was fine, he typed. When are you coming back? Patricio's ass sweated, the chair trembled in place. I don't know, probably not this semester, it's a four-month suspension, he replied, and reflexively punched the table from below, knocking over a glass that shattered on the tiles. All right, but come out of your cave. Okay okay, he told her, I'll stop by next week. Patricio, red-faced, brow beaded, contained himself and rewound the video, trying to synchronize his ejaculation with the actors'.

By the time Cata came home, Pato was asleep in his room. Cata went to wake him. She was hungry. He peeled his face from the pillow, damp with drool, and rubbed his eye with the knuckles of his right hand.

"There's nothing here, barata.[1] Have some water."

Catalina returned to the kitchen, shook off her backpack, and lifted a heavy five-liter jug of water to pour herself a glass. Then she dragged a chair from the living room, left it by the counter, set her backpack onto the seat, climbed onto it, and strained her arms until she managed to open, gingerly, with her fingertips, the doors of the highest cabinet. Balancing there, she found the package of Super 8 cookies that her dad had hidden from her.

When Patricio emerged, he found his sister asleep on the couch. The chocolate rouge around her lips made her look older, and yet her pose was innocent, unguarded. Patricio scanned the floor, found nothing. He went into the kitchen, shook the trash can. There they were, viscous shells, all clustered together, then exploding into swift ellipses like a set of black marbles. Pato caught a cockroach between his fingers and brought it close to his sister's face. The six leglets pumped in their frenzied dance.

"Wake up, baratita. Are you hungry?"

⚙

WHEN PEDRO STARTED working in the tree plantation, he was still so scrawny and inept that the ax blade snagged in the trunk on his first day. His squad partners cackled, applauded,

---

1 *Blatta orientalis:* a common insect, dark brown or black in color, that likes to dig between the fingers of the dead. <I couldn't find this part about dead bodies...surely the insect has other ways of surviving?

and thumped him on the back. Nice job, look at the skinny kid go, they hooted. Now try hauling that log on your shoulders. The foreman, seeing that he wasn't cut out for it, led him to the whip-sawyers. Then came an afternoon of shared effort, coordinating his pulls on the saw's rough handle with those of Astorga—a flabby asshole who called him kiddo, runt, fragile, puppy, soft palms, broken nail, splinter in delicate flesh—on the other side of the fallen tree. At the end of the day, his shoulders were stiff and his arms shuddered.

The boss doubled back on him at the exit.

"Hey, you know how to fill out a table?"

He'd spent weeks watching these men work. Barely acknowledged by the others, Pedro counted the logs they piled onto the truck bed, corroborating the number of trunks, ensuring they had no fewer rings than the mandatory minimum. There were laws. Only the old eucalyptuses could come down. The youngsters were to be left alone. In general, fifty, sometimes even eighty logs were loaded up and transported out, readied for cutting and cleaning. One afternoon, Pedro amused himself by imagining that the rings formed a language, that every ring spelled years of tree history and tree memories, like in photographs: classmates all lined up, sitting beside each other in class, swapping notes, whispering among themselves, chasing a ball at recess. That's what he was thinking about when a heavy log clipped him on the back of the head. The choker setters' laughter sank into his skin like a tattoo. Even the squad leader cackled. Pedro rubbed himself slowly and laughed too. Adjusted his helmet. Don't pay Astorga no mind, man, his coworkers said. He's a smart-ass, that's all, you get used to it. He listened to them, in his way: He lifted a rock and lobbed it at the porker's head.

After a month and a half of work, he was wrecked. The first few days were the worst. Following the men uphill through sun and shade, hands caked with dirt, nails blackened, fingertips adorned with so many splinters that there was no point in taking them out. The omnipresent pesticidal dust prompting coughs and sinus infections. A shared life. The fatso's jokes. His own languid persistence beneath them. His coworkers said he didn't have a sense of humor. Come on, Pedrito, it ain't nothing. He'd lower his arms, clutching his clipboard, eyes cast down behind the group. That's when he started gathering eucalyptus pods. He'd look for them on his lunch hour, select husks that were similar in shape and pierce each one in the same spot. He'd say to himself: Better a craftsman than a grunt.

Making matters worse, his wages were stolen at the end of the first month. He'd carefully tucked the bills into the bottom of his backpack, standing in the little alcove where Astorga shamelessly masturbated, threatening to spatter you if you watched or said anything. Come on, relax. No one else gives a shit, the axman Juan Carlos said to him. Why whine about it. On the evening he couldn't find the roll of blue bills inside his clean socks, he walked up into the brush until he was out of sight. He sat on a pine stump and tried not to cry, but he couldn't help it.

It was as if the world had stopped. Life was scarce in those plots of land, but so was silence. Expanses of sticks and twigs, dust, metal cables, sweaty glances, scribbles, simple fauna, withered flora, hole saws, the swift and rhythmic groan of wood growing into coffins, sawdust, men half asleep, cut fingers waving, hands bleeding onto the lichen, lush moss that doesn't grow much but peeks, sometimes, from the corners of mirrors and showers. It was as if the forest itself had hurled a rock at his head.

Pedro always limped a little after that episode. But the next week, he was trudging uphill with his clipboard again, ax over his shoulder, sweating, whistling. He'd joke back and chuckle.

Over time, he became one with his labor. His body adapted to the rigor of the days, arms and back gained muscle mass with every blow. His humor conformed to that of his fellows. He no longer made a fuss when someone cleaved his boots into a log at lunch. He'd hear them laughing and let the wind brush it off him, shoo away the forest heat, shifting the boughs of the pines and eucalyptuses, offering their sweet shade.

·ᛟ·

"THE MUSHROOM *Ganoderma lucidum* is a naturally wood-degrading saprotrophic basidiomycete, but it demonstrates a series of highly useful pharmacological effects. This, given the scarcity of the species in natural environments, has fostered the artificial cultivation of its fruiting bodies in specialized greenhouses by means of trunks or sawdust in bags and plastic bottles. The mushroom is characterized by its reddish, generally kidney-shaped cap, supported by a svelte foot in a slightly tortuous position. Its mycelium feeds on the dead wood of broad-leafed trees and contains a high concentration of triterpenes and polysaccharides, both prized pharmacological components. Useful properties against hepatitis and hypertension in triterpenes have been documented; so have anti-tumoral effects in polysaccharides. The latter have sparked considerable research interest in the *Ganoderma* genus among contemporary medical mycologists, as well as in the commercialization of its derivations in the alternative oncological therapy market."

Giovanna spoke with the steady cadence of an experienced lecturer. The fifty-seat auditorium was full, and the slide sequence marked the pulse of her presentation. This was one of the keynote addresses Giovanna would deliver throughout the year at universities across the country, a means of compensating the state for the fellowship she'd received to study abroad. She hated these activities: They reactivated her fear of standing at the blackboard in elementary school. Her adult academic work had forced her to get used to it, but it still felt clumsy and tedious, and she operated on autopilot, just fulfilling her duty.

At least academia allowed her to visit Concepción once in a while. She could see family, friends. Mechanically answer colleagues' questions about her research for the book she was writing.[2] Insist to her parents that she was fine on her own. That she'd gone on some dates, but nothing serious. English guys are boring, Mom. All they do is drink and talk about their work.

"Therapeutic uses of this mushroom can be traced back thousands of years in classical Chinese medicine, which called it *Lingzhi* and employed it primarily to alleviate fatigue, asthma, and liver disorders."

She observed the audience's faces as she spoke. Somewhere along the way, she'd learned to separate speech from thought, like someone who begins to disassociate the actions of their hands in learning to juggle. She quickly scanned some of the professors sitting in the first row. Middle-aged men with similar signs of degradation: baldness, paunches, facial creases, pinched expressions, shabby dress, poor hygiene, bad breath. One of their ilk had recently published a review that ridiculed her dissertation.

She also focused on a student in the third row. Her blond side-shaved hair was drawn back with a bow, and she studied Giovanna intently, legs crossed, taking notes.

Giovanna's presentation concluded with an emphasis on how science, confronting an uncertain future, finds fertile

---

2 She did this innocently, my girl. Writing down ideas that would unwittingly bring to bear dark consequences, for thoughts are no more than an unknowable design. She was following something that gusted up at her from down below, from the loose earth of the white brain.

ground in researching the fungus kingdom and its prodigious properties. She showed a sequence of slides on the use of mushrooms as fuel, plastic-degrading products, selective pest control, antidepressants, anticarcinogens, and producers of the most powerful antibacterial enzymes on record.

Half an hour later, Giovanna found herself in conversation by the refreshment table with a group of biology students. As if trying to mask her reticence, the note-taking girl now looked her right in the eye as Giovanna spoke.

"The truth is, we know very little about fungi. Their life cycles are strange, and although they don't look it, they're more like us than like bacteria or the plant kingdom. Invasive, authoritarian creatures. Extremely intelligent. Let's take *Entomophthora muscae*, for example, a parasitic fungus that infects the housefly. Contagion occurs when the fungal spores land and germinate on top of it, penetrating its exoskeleton. According to the research, the first thing the fungus does is advance into the fly's brain and seize control of its movements. It settles in the neural area in charge of the feet and wings, forcing it to alight on some nearby surface and climb to its highest point. Eventually, the fungus drops the fly. Its wings don't react. The insect hits the ground, paralyzed. Then the hyphae of the fungus start to digest its innards, and the fly dies. Tiny cracks open in its body and sporangia sprout: countless tiny spore-sacs ready to embark in search of new flies."

⚙

HE STARED OUT the window of the truck, following the undulations of the power lines. This was sailing, he thought. A boat in the middle of the night, a mile from shore. He remembered his time as a fisherman. His father would take him out in the motorboat when he was little, perched between his legs like a favorite cabin boy. He'd close his eyes when he felt queasy and let drowsiness overtake him. Sometimes he'd rest his head against his father's belly and sleep awhile. Those were their closest moments. Things were different on land.

As a child, Pedro lived with his dog Chicho and his father in a house in the woods. They had everything a peasant farmer could need. His mother had died in childbirth and her face faded in his mind after they lost, along with the house, the only surviving photo of her. One September night, a truck of soldiers pulled up, pounded on the door, and led his father outside. He had to go, they told him. The farm was now the property of Araucana Timber Enterprises. But I bought this land from the cooperative! I own this house! Then the soldier, a kid with a hideous nose, shoved him against the wall. Pedro came out to throw his teenage body into the fray. They took his dog. Flung it at the wall and shot.

Pedro's dad sank low and then lower after he lost the property in Curanilahue.[3] He headed north, found work as a

---

3 "Rocky ford" in Mapudungun. Because the soil is packed with pebbles even in the cemetery. They're uncomfortable underfoot, don't let you rest. That's why the thread arranges them over time, to distance them from each sunken body, then drink from it.

gardener. He rented a little house on a little plot. He'd sit in the dirt to drink. Young Pedro would help him, pouring out his booze, draping him in a blanket, dragging him back to his cot. No animals, no garden, no friends. A single straight line from work to drink. The son endured two years before he retreated south. That was when he got the job at the tree plantation.

Before the Sudoku books, Pedro whiled away the empty hours gathering eucalyptus pods, collecting insects in his lunchbox—damselflies, ladybugs, beetles—making small talk with Gómez the caliber operator, bantering with Araya, the old coal seller. They went way back, hiking up to the clearings side by side, Pedro marking the size of the logs as the other man sawed, talking about soccer, about their kids, sitting around at lunch, finding a spot to nap. Araya's always been good with Catita, he said to María once, but she shook her head, blew into her coffee. Listen to me, she said, don't let that guy take the girl to school ever again, and a line of cold darted up his back, rage into his shoulders, the cup steaming on the table, the TV mute, and then Pedro stopped talking to him, they made their measurements in silence, Araya's head down, clearing the slings from the trunks, Pedro whistling so he wouldn't have to speak, so Araya won't ask him a thing, he'll kill him if he does.

He talked and talked with María, always, about everything, the news, horoscopes, sick dad in La Calera, alone, Pato's friends, those flies, about the company soccer tournament, careful you, your knee's still shaky, yes, María, yes, tomorrow, buttercup, about the strike, about the union, those fuckers from La Mutual, about yet another Mapuche kid murdered by the cops, yeah, another one, how is it possible, was he young?, just a baby, ay María. He made her necklaces she wore as bracelets, they ate dinner together, watching TV, she'd have the food ready when he got out of the shower, both hungry, come here, sit by me, two little pats on the sofa cushion, then others against the naked back, María, her cheeks red when the kids were asleep and the barking dogs let them make noise, give themselves permission, careful or you'll knock over the lamp, Pedrito, and smoking, María, she always smoked in bed, and he told jokes and stories that only he found funny, almost always about his dad, always dumb, like the time he fled from the cops on horseback, full moon, drunk as a skunk, the lights on the squad car trailing him through the woods, him leaping over a gorge, or when, in failing to respect the right of way, a transit cop discovered two open bottles of grappa sitting pretty in the passenger seat. He laughed and María smoked slowly, gazing out the window, listening to the dogs settle in for the night, coordinating her sleepiness with the kids'.

That was until she got sick.

There had to be a reason, but who knows. Maybe it was because they started buying their food in the city, because the tree plantation kept draining near the house, because the harvest was meager, because the garden dried out, because they had to sell part of the land parcel, because the hens were listless and all but stopped laying, because the water was toxic, because the kids needed notebooks to write in, Pedrito, textbooks for studying, because we'd better get Cata's diabetes treated, because Pato won't want to see me like this, take care of the bees for me, because you know how things are, something grabs us by the throat and doesn't let go and it's all so fast you don't have time to figure out how to face it, get ready, body and soul, how to say goodbye, let alone carry on, hauling logs heavy as a coffin on his shoulders, splintering him deep, because sometimes the air gets denser and the nights are long with breathing.

☼

"**WHAT'S MY PRINCESS** drawing today?" Pedro asked, peering over his daughter's shoulder.

"Us," she said, and pointed to her notebook. "That's me, this is you, and that's Pato."

The drawing, which she'd made in colored pencil, showed three stick figures with large heads and a range of expressive faces. The one farthest to the right had electrified hair, hands spread open, its tongue stuck out, and two *x*'s for eyes. The one in the middle had a strange flower emerging from behind the head, rising up to the edge of the page. The one to the left had its eyes closed as if deep in slumber.

"Beautiful, love," Pedro said, and gave her a kiss on the forehead.

"It's for you," Catalina replied. She tore the page from the notebook and her father tucked it away in his backpack.

☼

THEY NESTLED TOWARD the left. Rain streamed silently outside. If you paid attention, it was there, present. If you talked, you couldn't hear it anymore. Giovanna curled her body closer to Andrea's, pressed a hand to her chest, and asked her, innocent:

"Is it possible to put a person under a microscope?"

"How?"

"Like a whole person. Can you imagine seeing all their cells moving around at the same time?"

For a few seconds, neither said a word. Giovanna closed her eyes. Heard the rain. On a different night, she'd once confessed to someone that she felt, in moments like these, her thoughts slipping right out of her. She loved that. It was one of her favorite things.

"I don't know. Maybe a big enough lens could do it," Andrea said.

"Really?"

"I don't get it. What's your point?"

They spoke slowly, skin warm under their T-shirts. Giovanna brushed a hand across Andrea's forehead. She opened and closed her eyes with every sound. Talking meant being awake. Soon, they'd sleep. There was no rush. They could say everything more easily, unguarded. She focused on her own pulse and the rain eased the weight of thinking.

"There's something I want to know," Giovanna said.

"What?"

"What can you feel?"

"Now?"

"Yeah."

"The rain. Your voice behind me."

"What else?"

"Heat in my stomach. Your hand on my chest. The edge of your knee against my thigh. Your nose at my neck. Your breathing."

"What else?" Giovanna said, unfolding her body above her.

"Why do you ask?"

"There's something I want to know."

Their words spread like moss between them.

"What?"

Giovanna turned toward her and pulled her close.

"If you can feel your own skin."

·☼·

WITH MARÍA GONE, Pedro was different. His mood had left with her, his coworkers would say. He didn't care. He had his kids and all his fingers, and except for a slight limp in his left knee, his body worked just fine.

His luck was foreign to many of his fellows. Juan Carlos was a reminder of this: the scar on his chin. And José, known as Cat Paw, who'd lost the upper phalanxes of his right hand, which he now used only to hold a clipboard. Saws were serious business. Some of the old guys, like Pedro, respected them. These fuckin blades, he'd mutter to Juan Carlos. The devil eats the metal. Then he'd look at young Carrasco sawing

away and recall years of sheer axes, when fewer fingers flew
and the trees could admire, attentively, their cesarean scars.

Later, when they both climbed into the company truck,
Pedro would pit old against new in his head: his own oak
plot versus this new drunken, subcontracted time. He'd gaze
at the machines. Those huge, wheeled arms, strong enough to
chop and strip dozens of hectares in a single day. What could
you do? Five of his crew's workdays amounted to the yield
of a sole machine technician. Pedro coughed. He'd eaves-
drop on the owners of the tree plantation. They never tired
of prattling about their acquisitions, praising them shamelessly before the workers they would soon fire. Every so often,
he'd picture Mr. John Deere at his desk, opening the drawer
where he kept a bottle of liquor, the cigars he smoked as he
listened to jazz. On other afternoons, he'd watch the har-
vester effortlessly uproot a eucalyptus, scrape the bark, and
add it to the pile, so that the world could develop a taste for
dry soil in the throat, the town could soak in booze, corners
cut shorter, ground parched beneath them as they came and
went, colliding, drowsy, cleaved with splinters, hands gashed
by circular saws, band saws, wood edgers, while his children,
dazed, made their first slashes in the notebooks that marked
their entrance into language: kit-ty, big-tree, ma-ma, give-me
a-no-ther coo-kie, the-lake-went-dry.

Pedro cut as if his cough didn't exist. He ignored it, mis-
took it for the drone of the chainsaw. A cough can be disre-
garded for a while, but at the end of the day it's like a debt. It

had gotten worse and everyone was telling him so. Marambio, you gotta take care of that, Juan Carlos would urge. You sound like a dog about to kick the bucket.

When lunch hour rolled around, he'd slip deeper into the woods, far from the rest of the crew. He'd look for a kindly stump or trunk, a bit of shade. The ground coated in withered ochre leaves, crunching with every step. It wasn't easy to shed the sun out there: The heat seemed to climb up from the earth. The forest is angry at that time of day. It chafes at people. Come on, man, stay and eat with us, Juan Carlos would insist. But he wouldn't listen.

He'd do his Sudoku puzzles over lunch. He was about to finish the hard level and he felt proud. He considered what it must have been like to invent a game like that. Imagined some bored Japanese guy staring out the window of an office building, sketching grids and numbers on fogged glass as rain fell on the other side.[4] If he himself had been capable of coming up with such a thing, he thought, he would have. A simple, noble form of entertainment that crossed entire continents, like wood. He'd fill the page, sweating as if he had a fever, wiping his face and hands with a napkin. Every number is a tree, he'd tell himself. You have to put it in place and let it grow. Once the page is full, the forest comes down. Then the next page: more blank squares.

---

4 Because the poor idiot didn't know it was invented by Leonhard Euler, an eighteenth-century Swiss mathematician.

But the cough went about its funerary functions. Between spoonfuls, Pedro struggled to breathe. He set down the notebook and brought his right fist to his mouth. Blood. Red phlegm with white spots on his hand. Panic. Trying to stand, he overturned the little tin pot, stumbled, and fell, hands sinking into eucalyptus leaves and beans with pork and pasta. Eyes red. More coughing, retching. He was too far from the group, it was no use. His body mud-smeared, crouched on all fours, desperate to take in oxygen. The scent of hot food, the vomited rind and mashed noodles. The dry earth clouding his face, turning to clay on his cheeks. A shout, muffled, but by whom.

When they found him, his vital signs were weak. When Patricio appeared at the clinic, his father was hooked up to a respirator.

‑ϙ‑

PATRICIO WAS A TREE TRUNK. He stood beside the hospital bed, completely detached from the sound, eyes fixed on a thin, transparent plastic tube in his father's mouth. A doctor was speaking behind him and a nurse placed a hand on his right shoulder, a gesture he couldn't feel. His body had been pressed out of the world; he received their words like coins tossed into a fountain. He was focused on Pedro's face, on the sheets covering him from chest to toe. He sat for four hours by the bed. He watched TV, listless. The rhythm of the respirator distressed him. The tubes full of condensation, drops of blood, fresh breath, false breath. The room's asepsis marked by the ticking of the clock. Something random on TV, a morning show, music videos, news of a scarlet fever outbreak in Barcelona, some attack in France, disturbances in downtown Santiago, the announcement of forest fire season that periodically menaced the sleep of the eucalyptus children, as pale and dehydrated as Pedro and the four others from that doomed work crew, intubated in neighboring rooms of the hospital as their kids begged them not to stay asleep forever.

He wondered if they'd cut him open somewhere. If breathing this way meant you were more a body or more a puppet. If he could hear his son talking to him. The sun lit the plastic tube, exposing the dense air inside. The doctor explained things, curtly and then at length, but Patricio couldn't process the information. What worried him was his sister. What time did she get out of school? What would she think when she came home to an empty house?

He asked the nurse about the next visiting hours, thanked her with a nod, and left the room.

The bus dropped him off outside the school. Sweating, he waited for her. Hey, let's go. What's wrong? Nothing, kid, let's walk. Why are you shaking? I'm not, hurry up. I'm hungry. Along the way, he made up a story about Pedro having to go visit Aunt Carmela, who'd tripped while rearranging the furniture, broken her shoulder, had to rest in bed. That Dad had offered to look after her. He'd be home at night, maybe later. No, he didn't say when. So she should sit and let him cook. And if she had homework they'd do it together. Did she want pasta or rice with her hot dog.

As Cata napped, he logged onto the computer. Messaged some friends. Put on a black windbreaker and went out. Bought some beers from the corner store and walked to the park. He found them on the playground.

The air grew damp as night fell. They smoked three joints among the four of them, poorly rolled, coughing hard, laughing like horses, downing six liters as they swung from the monkey bars, simulating Olympics and races on the exercise machines. The test went like this: Each one mounted an elliptical and they'd see who lasted longest while pushing the yellow bars as hard as they could. Eyes closed, Patricio felt his body curve and levitate, as if at any moment he might stumble and wake up again at school, at the interregional soccer championship, sleeping in a bus that stank of defeat, in the truck riding home with his dad, an arm around Cata, sitting very close to each other like a pair of backpacks, needing to pee, his body finally out of the pool, swinging a punch at the cousin who'd shoved him into the water, biting the neck of his first girlfriend, crying at the slam of a soccer ball to the stomach, standing beside a totaled bicycle, a door crushed against a finger, solving problems in a notebook, slouching at the blackboard to present his work, teaching long division to his sister, jacking off in a bathroom stall, in his grandmother's bed, at the kitchen table, stoned on the bus from Curanilahue to Concepción, head dropped onto a plate of pasta, puke everywhere, crashing into the door of a bar, destroying a bus stop, falling asleep and waking up at the station in another city, hot, pulling himself together after scoring an own goal, wiping his face on the neck of his T-shirt, the reek of sweat and shame, as his father slept on the couch, still dressed, tray resting on his belly, eyebrows speckled with sawdust, stubble, grieving María, her cosmetics pouch hidden in a bathroom drawer, medications on her nightstand, jars of honey, her purse packed with underwear, notepads, Kleenex, little cases, photos, lipstick, her voice sounding abruptly from the kitchen, as if she were coming this way, as if in his dreams they could still talk to each other, he could still ask her how are you, Mama, I'm fine, dear heart, nothing hurts anymore, I miss you, I miss you too, love, his head suddenly unpeeled from the pillow, from the clammy pool on the cloth, flies wheeling in the heat of his room, forgetting the force of his body against the metal of the world, his father's white bed, and his friends, weaker, wasted, arms and legs spent, and him unscathed, stoic, martial, eyes still shut, hands steady, legs trembling, clutching the bars as if running and running could keep him in that faraway ellipse for longer.

·ọ·

PEDRO PUSHED THE WOODEN DOOR, sticky at the hinge, and the stale air struck him in the face. A chicken darted between his legs, restoring herself to the light after who knows how

many days indoors. His father was sitting on the floor, leaning against the back wall. Heat bowed, chin to chest.

"Hey, Pops..."

From the old man's mouth streamed a derisive line of spit-
tle. In the bubbles gathered at his collar there rose a heavy,
uncomfortable murmur. Pedro covered his nose. Grabbed
his father by the armpits and dragged him out of the room,
scattered with bottles that rolled around the dirt floor.

Once the old man was lying on the ground outside, Pedro
went for a bucket—it had a few bugs stuck to the bottom—
and flung the cold water onto him.

"Motherfuuuucker!"

The shrill voice startled the hens pecking nearby. Pedro
tried not to laugh. "Dad, can you hear me?"

"What the fuck is happening?" His words came out damp
and ponderous. Eyes fixed to the ground.

"You seen María? Did she come through here?"

The old man recovered a bit of his composure and sat up,
shaking out his hair, brushing at his soaked shirt. His eyes
were sunken into his face's red well deep. He lurched past the
chickens, which craned their necks by the open door, flailing
at the air, muttering his geezery gripes, and slammed it shut.

"NO, AUNT CARMELA isn't better yet. Maybe tomorrow."

Catita was asking after her father over breakfast and the
first thing Patricio did was lie to her. The TV set showed a
busted background from the poor signal. He got up to switch

it off, deciding the antenna was beyond repair. He told Cata to hurry up or she'd be late for school.

Back at home, he logged on. A classmate messaged him to ask when was he coming out to party again, everyone was forgetting what he looked like. Patricio replied with a meme and closed Facebook. He Googled comas.

His first discovery was that he'd never thought about how a word could have multiple meanings. Although the first Wikipedia article he clicked on—"Comma"—wasn't the one he wanted, there was a series of concepts that briefly held his interest. Sentence. Conjunctions. Conjunctive adverb. Phrase. Vocative. Predicate. He clicked on another article. "Coma." He found the medical definition of the term. For an instant, he remembered a foot peeking out from under the white hospital sheet. A stiff, odorless toe, rubbery. The concept in question came from the Greek and meant "deep slumber."[5] A coma may be caused by poisoning (from alcohol, drugs, or toxins), cardiac arrest, metabolic anomalies, central nervous

---

5 Although it thinned him out, dreaming made Pedro no less vivid. Such a verb only means remaining more present than in death. Centuries back, Hippo, the philosopher, saw his wife fall into a ditch and lie prostrate, catatonic. One afternoon, watching her sleep, he thought that dreams must be made of water: external light enters them and refracts, producing the images that surround the slumberer. The time of dreams is so much water: a wide lake for the mind to swim in. His wife soon died, but he knew what he had to do to find her. One morning, he tied a eucalyptus crown around his head and six heavy stones around his waist, and he threw himself off a cliff into the waters of the Ionian Sea.

system abnormalities, strokes, traumatic brain injuries, seizures, hypoxia, and other untranslatable conditions. Coma. A small mark, a faint tear that isolates speech, pauses, gives air, allows thinking to stretch, to reinforce its limits, a respite for an eye weary of seeing, the aberration inherent to certain optic systems, a serious loss of consciousness. Pointless. Why even try to come up with your own diagnosis when there was so much to read. Even thinking was pointless. Imagination was exhausting, discouraging. Patricio opened other medical websites, news stories, discussion forums. Floods of information. Nowhere did he find anything about what was happening to his father.

Hunger led him by the hand into the kitchen. He opened the fridge, took out an old block of cheese in dubious condition. He stuffed it into a white roll and poured himself a glass of the remaining beer. The look in his eyes, stale as the drink, narrowed slowly, then blackened into a dream as he slept on the couch, back turned to the room.

He dreamed he was dying. A white sheet engulfed him. He drooled onto the cushion for several minutes, paralyzed, in limbo. He tried to scream, his body stiff, face slick as he felt himself floating down the river. He thought he'd gotten infected by visiting Pedro. That his organs would soon succumb to a sudden, fatal virus. He thought about whether he'd been a good son or bad. He thought of Cata and his mom. He thought of them both. The names of several women passed through his mind without affixing to a face, a body, a voice.

He strained to see the house, the living room around him, felt a pang of sorrow, then nothing. He closed his eyes, surrendered to the dream. A watery voice called out to him. All he saw was the color green. He heard a name, a warm voice at his ear. He looked at his hands, turned to water. In a mirror, his reflection was translucent, as if his skin were made of wicker. He heard the voice inside. His feet stood on damp ground, like the bottom of a dry lake. He stared down and saw his father. His father's face multiplied hundreds of thousands of times. Eyes open alongside radiant numbers and signs, written in rows and boxes. A vast, moss-green space. The eyes spoke to each other, staring at him. In the midst of all that, his body was a dot. A brief air. Terrified, he struggled, trying to wrest his feet from the ground so he could run, leaving the forest far behind, but he turned entirely to water and woke up.

⚙

GIOVANNA SHUT THE NOTEBOOK. She was spending a few days in Valdivia to work on a mushroom-cataloging project, a commission from Austral University. Sitting by the woodstove, she reviewed her notes from that afternoon, copied some she thought might be relevant to her book. She was engrossed until Andrea's voice called to her from the second floor of the cabin.

Some notes speculated:

> The mushroom is red, gelatinous in texture, exactly like a gumdrop. I found this *Guepiniopsis alpina* on the trunk of a fallen peumo tree. The wood's pale gray

skin is corpse-like. The roots are exposed. The start of the trunk, hollow, rotten. But its essence seems contained in that gelatin. It's not for nothing that certain gummies in Chile are called "substances."

❖

The common name for another mushroom in the same family, but with a different color, is "elf shit." Mucilaginous mushroom that forms plasmodium, an ameboid mass that moves on its own. Its other common name is "dog vomit." I've found it on the ground, generally covered in dry leaves or plant residue and on decomposed wood. Cosmopolitan. Yellow. They're also mobile, small amoeba advancing along rotten myrtle trunks. Don Carlos helps me with some stories. Andrea talks with him and he loves it, she's so friendly, it gets him going. He's the park ranger. He doesn't let us come in with food. He asks us to hand over our water bottles. Everything stays at reception. I hide this notebook in my windbreaker. I forget the weed in the banana tree. Farther south, he tells us, the elf shit marks the presence of the Trauco goblin.

❖

The *Guepiniopsis,* or "forest gumdrop," is typically eaten by a small beetle from the Tenebrionidae family, recently cataloged as genus *Heliofugus.* I come into possession of a specimen I find right by my shoe (what would have become of me if I'd stepped on it), hidden among some leaves. I place it in my hand. Andrea and I examine it, play around, put it into photographic perspective. Fascinated, we're like two bugs emerging from a jar to take in the world. The edge is narrow glass. You can smell it.

⚙

Aextoxicon punctatum. The olivillo tree. Olivillo. What a nice word. The tongue pushes its sound through the nose. I read that its fruits ripen like small black olives. But the name is deceptive: They're not olives and the trunks are huge.

⚙

On the bark of a cinnamon tree I notice a proliferation of nodules that look like signs, or stretch marks. I wonder what kind of language lives there. Who it speaks to. The bark is high in vitamin C. But what does this property mean for the hypothesis? I touch a finger to the trunk. I confess my secret, scrape it, think in Braille. Maybe I can read it. I receive nothing. She comes looking for me. I'd hung back, taking photos. The light cuts diagonally across the hieroglyphics. We follow the trail, talking about the possibility of a graphic language, a language more of the eye than of the ear.

⚙

We reach the end of the olivillo forest in Curiñanco, which is also the last stretch of highway from Valdivia to Niebla, and now I'm sitting at the end point of the path through the park. I look up at the treetops, thirty, forty meters above. What can any measurement do with this kind of vastness? That's the trouble with analogizing immensity. If you say something's as big as the moon or the ocean, it's just not the same: No one can get their head around it. It's hard to find a precise enormity. I watch her standing at the lookout. Her small frame next to mine, magnificent under the trees. I love how her loose hair offers me glimpses of the ocean in the distance, the subtle movements she makes to comb it. There's grandeur in finding the proper scale. The olivillo trunks make us crane our necks and straighten our posture as we walk. All I want is this expansion of air when we take in the heights. I see them and picture my lungs as an elastic organ, imagine my breath moving through me to touch her, drinking from her own. I picture myself for an instant as a tree trunk reaching toward the light. I want to show her that I'm hers, the very same species connected underneath, as the sun passes over the surf and our trunks age, united, for a couple centuries more.

☼

IN WINDY WEATHER, leaves gusting about, volatile enough that he constantly had to zip and unzip his sweatshirt, and to think a lot, Patricio left the house behind. His jogging pants, old and ripped down the right side, grew spattered with dirt.

The erosion, the splintered earth, began before the sign that said TIMBER PLANTATION. Patricio climbed the slope with the help of a long stick. He liked reaching the electric fence, taking in the formidable enclosure. They've been made like this for some time: tall barriers traversed by bird-crisping cable. He squinted to the other side. Wondered how long it would take for the men working several kilometers beyond to make their way here, to cut down this part of the forest.

Remember that walk to Trongol Alto where you shat in my arms and Mom got mad at me for almost dropping you when I tried to cover my nose? That languid humidity on his cheeks, the scent of moss, of loose digüeñe mushrooms, feet sucked down into the clay, ankle rash from the nettles, the whispers of the peumo trees concealing foxes and pudus that lurched away from us, skin radiant in the cold, when there wasn't yet a fence to cross and the wet woods were full of changle mushrooms and loyo mushrooms and other mushrooms Mom taught us to forage for—remember what all of that was like before these fake logs?

He talked to himself. The eucalyptus trees repeated themselves like mirrors ricocheting with sun, and he licked his cracked lips. The burning heat nagged at him, made him picture himself in the middle of the Pacific, floating in a skiff for days. There was dirt stuck to the corner of his mouth. Stubble sparse but growing, a patch of grubby hair. In his shoes, his skin hid his affinity for other kingdoms. His feet itched. Last night he'd tugged strips of white skin from between his toes. The sun crossed the woods, slipped into the streams and the hearts of thrushes, drank from slopes, swamps, and pools, dried out the eyes of owls strung from the electric fence. He wondered when it had last rained—was it before his father's coma?

A dead cow among the trees. Patricio approached and inspected it carefully, like someone using their fingers to zoom in on a photograph. Its jaw was broken, dangling like a strip of jerky. Hide sealed against the bone. An open horn sheltered a family of flies, which worked little and slowly and that was that. The rest was left to the sun. Neither ants nor mushrooms felt like going in to disassemble. Repulsed, he beheld the scene. It sickened him that the cow had no smell. All the dead animals he'd encountered always left a several-day sensory memento, a courtesy that led him, by its absence, back to his father's body. That dry skin, eroding all by itself in the hospital room, while an external pulse charged his lungs. He felt a rush of rage and desolation and wanted to cry and wanted it to rain so that no one could distinguish the two actions on his face. He gave the cow's head a hard kick, and a rectangular scrap of jaw flew a few meters into the air, casting up dust where it fell.

He kept walking. More bugs and dead birds. It was as if the entire hectare had been cleared by a kind of taxidermy, blotting his recollection of drinking boldo leaf tea by the wood-burning kitchen, where he once heard his mother pray to Saint Michael the Archangel for rain. His nose filled with the reek of dust and eucalyptus. He blew it like a soccer player, wiped his hand on his pants, and kept his pace, staring ahead.

☼

THE PINE NEEDLES scratched his face. Someone had to push the heavy branches forward as someone else lifted the wire fence. Where am I? Pedro wondered. People passed them one by one. He trailed the others. He had some blankets slung over his shoulder, a water jug in one hand. His friend Juan Carlos led the way, tugging at a mule laden with cargo. Old and wily, the animal tried to take an uphill detour through the weeds. Juan Carlos wasn't strong enough. His face and arms looked like a boy's.

"Come on now!" whispered an old woman's voice from behind, rebuking Juan Carlos in his daze. "Put your back into it!"

As he watched his friend's figure growing more childlike with every pull, he thought about the days of the peasant farmer cooperatives, a story he'd heard from his father. The images returned to him now, cast onto the expanse of the meadow and the skirts of the Nahuelbuta mountains, like slides under the moon's flickering light. Suddenly, the view was a single shared plot of land. He advanced among translucent men, women, and children all around him, carrying foodstuffs and construction materials, and passed a few old men seated farther out, playing cards over an elm stump, drinking fresh chicha, where the midday sun interrupted these shifting shadows, inviting him to unbutton his shirt and clap as they collected the cards and money. This world filed past his own and he feared the aperture. Could I be dead, if they're greeting me but not touching me? he wondered, as he felt something bite him between the toes.

The old woman shoved his back. The other group, opaque, walked on, intent on their mission. Juan Carlos's hazy double had a firmer grip on the stirrups between his arms, which had grown more adult. Pedro stood still, looking down at his hands.

Juan Carlos turned his head and told him to hurry up. His eyes were clouded. We're almost there, he said, pointing at the fence that blocked the path a few kilometers off. That's the New World.

Pedro stopped short.

"Excuse me, have you seen a woman passing through? Dark skin, about my build. Sometimes she wears her hair in a braid with a blue clip," he said in a voice that didn't sound like his own.

But the farmers marched on, heads bowed. A violet light shone on their faces, which glanced ahead before returning abruptly to the ground, as if by spring action. They were dragging goods that seemed to have survived a fire. Then Pedro saw two children lugging a half-charred mattress, along with a TV set, blankets, a table and chairs, a washing machine, two bicycles, a black barking dog, a couple of books, and some work tools.

"Hey, buddy, have you heard anything about my wife?"

He tried to tap the boy on the shoulder, but his hand passed through as if touching water.

Then the boy asked his sister to stop. They set the mattress on the ground and looked at Pedro, who gathered his courage and continued.

"Her name is María. María Lemún."

⚙

ONE MORNING, THREE KITTENS appeared by the chicken coop. Catalina fell in love with them instantly. She put down the bowl of eggs she was gathering for breakfast and went to see. It was Saturday, around noon, and her brother wasn't up yet. She'd gotten tired of banging on his bedroom door.

She found the kittens squeezed in a corner, half hidden by a wooden board, a length of wire mesh, and a scrap of old metal. If she reached out a hand, the cats hissed, their instincts primed. Hardly able to walk, the three tiny creatures were already defending themselves from the world. It was when Catalina tried to pick one up that the mother emerged. Half black, half white, skinny, territorial. She charged, hackles raised, and the frenzied chickens scattered. In the chaos of dust and feathers, Catalina fell backward onto the eggs, staining her dress. The mother cat leapt away, watching everything. As Cata stood and tried to wipe off her clothes, she realized that one of the broody hens was missing. She went into the house. She knocked again, harder now, until Pato opened.

"Look what I found."

He was greeted by two crusty eyes, half open, barely able to receive the light. The startled kitten spread its tiny paws in hopes of clinging to the air, or releasing itself from Cata's clutches.

"What's this?" Pato plucked the kitten into his arms and stroked its nose.

"It was behind the coop. I took it and the mommy cat didn't notice."

"The chicken coop?" he shrilled. "Cata, for fuck's sake." And he ran out of the house in his red checkered boxers and black Metallica T-shirt. His bare feet kicked up dust until he reached the wire mesh that the cat was trying to wriggle under as the panicked hens flapped.

"Get out, you motherfucker! Out, you fucking cat!"

For an instant, the cat's eyes met his, utterly open and enraged, until Patricio's kick sent her flying over her young. Terrified, the kittens watched from a corner of the coop, heads wobbling, fur puffed.

Cata wept behind him, beat her fists against his back, her blows as soft as rounds from a peashooter. Stupid, stupid, Pato! I hate you! But two hours later she was asking him which name he liked best for the littlest cat, Chalkboard or Butter, I mean look at her, white white white with black spots like the butter you left outside and then it got covered in flies, Patricio chasing her around with a butter knife spread with bug-speckled fat, his sister shrieking in a white voice, the cat darting and skittering behind them, toppling mugs, spraying fleas, growing slowly but surely as its mother got pregnant again and lay in wait in the very same spot.

☼

HIS MOTHER DID SOMETHING with Catalina that Patricio envied intensely. She'd curl up next to the little girl and say blow, love, blow hard, okay, get it all out, let's have it all out and I'll keep it for you. She'd lay a hand on her forehead, take a deep breath, and ask God for the sickness to leave the child's body and enter hers instead. If it was His will for someone to suffer, she thought that person should be her, not her daughter. This act of love made Catalina cry—not with feeling, but with fear. I don't want you to die, Mama, she'd sob, enraging her brother as he spied on them, ears hot against the door.

Patricio remembered this as he tracked the pulse in his father's gaunt body, vein-fed, oxygenated by machines of uncertain prognosis. The nurses came and went to answer the questions of the few relatives who fretted briefly over Pedro and his children before forgetting about them again.

Aunt Carmela, for example, showed up to spend a weekend with the kids. As soon as she set foot in the house, she scolded Pato for not telling her anything and filling his sister's head with nonsense. Do you have shit for brains? Go lie down, she said, and as he walked toward his room, she repeated that if he treated Cata that way ever again, she'd call the police. As it turned out, there was no second visit: Their aunt made a break for it on Monday morning. She'd started the day screaming and flailing her arms when she found her bed filled with insects that scuttled all over her limbs and followed her into the shower, where a jet of cold water expelled them at last. Her nephew offered to see her to the bus stop. No need, she insisted, hair damp, still shaking, before she disappeared into the early morning mist. Patricio flung a box of cookies crawling with baratas into the yard, then went to wake Cata for breakfast.

He wondered if his mother was watching all this. If she was floating above the room or below it. He remembered her beekeeping phase. Months of seeing her all suited up like an astronaut, stepping outside to stun worker bees using a smoker filled with rosemary, rue, bay, and eucalyptus. María would pass her hands over the hive as her son peered out from indoors, imagining spoonfuls of fresh honey smeared onto bread.

Strange days followed. Dead bees cupped in her hands. A dry cough. A subtler tone in Pedro.

Patricio stared through the hospital window.

"I can feel you there, Mama. Please make Dad open his eyes."

·❀·

"YES?"

"Giovanna Oddó?"

"Speaking."

"I'm sorry to be calling so late, but it's urgent. This is Dr. Martín Moreno." The voice on the other end sounded as if it were underwater. Giovanna rubbed her eyes to hear better. "Could you come first thing to the Provincial Hospital of Curanilahue?"

Giovanna set three alarms on her cell phone and went back to sleep.

She drove to Curanilahue in the pre-dawn blue. The deserted highway helped her conjure hypotheses for the case. She remembered visiting another hospital to examine a baby girl with candidiasis so severe that her body was covered in red blotches and her tongue had gone white. How did they find me? she wondered, trying to recall whether her number appeared on any of the articles she'd published online. Then she passed two trucks ablaze. They looked like pachyderm corpses on the shoulder of the highway.

When she reached the modest hospital, she found Dr. Moreno waiting outside, smoking and fidgeting. He greeted her and asked her to accompany him into a lab room. The young doctor occasionally passed a hand over his head, as if to make sure his hair was still in place, using the other to click files on an old computer. They took ages to open.

"Here it is. This is what I need to show you," he said at last, resolute, as an image slipped down the screen like a curtain:

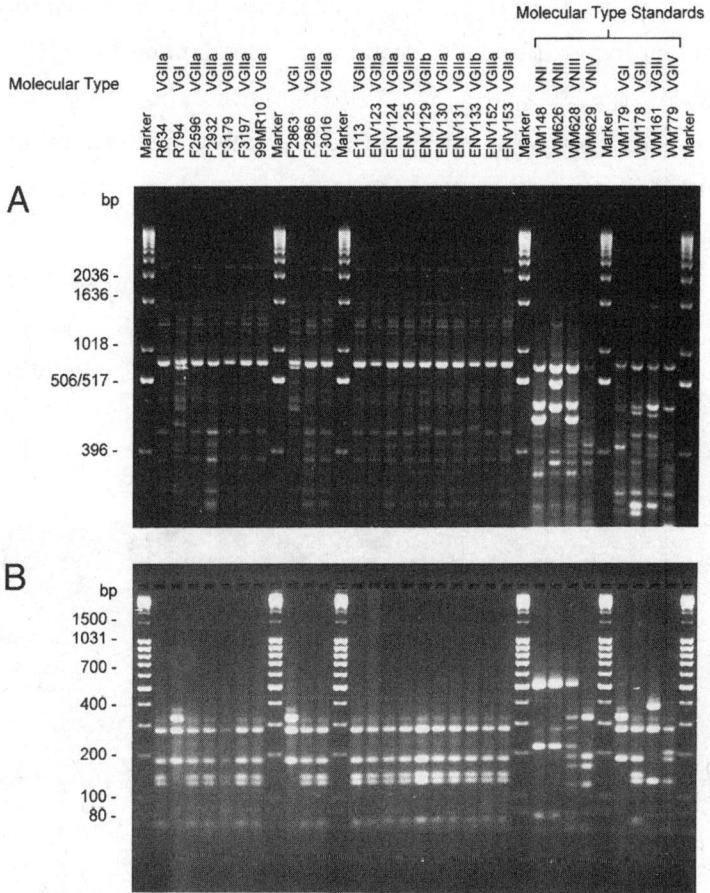

Giovanna, not understanding why they'd made her drive an hour and a half just to look at a file they could have emailed, leaned closer to the screen and focused in utter silence for several minutes.

"Is this person alive?" she asked.

"He was in a coma for over a month. The other infected individuals all died last week. We'll go up to see him shortly."

Unable to sleep that night, Giovanna opened her laptop. She propped a couple of cushions and straightened her back. She decided to analyze Dr. Moreno's information using more advanced software, hoping she'd get drowsy as the data rendered. But once the visualization was ready, the nagging voice in her head only grew louder.

Giovanna stared intently at the white markings, perplexed by how they could organize themselves in such a way. Thinking there must be a file error, she executed the operation again while making herself a cup of tea. The scene was identical when she returned.

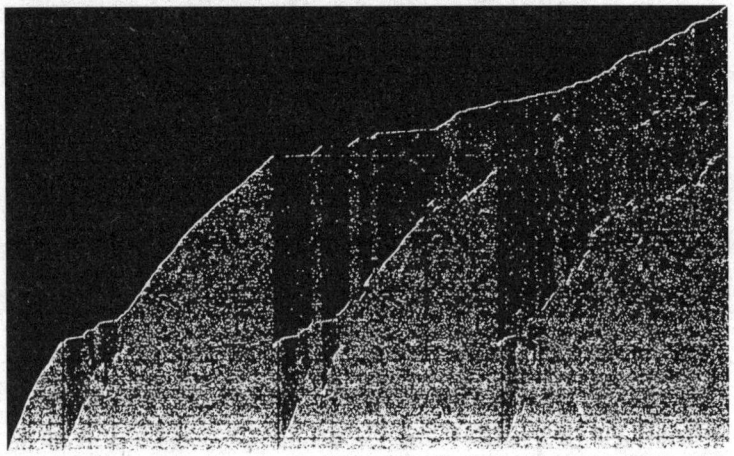

Nothing was in its right place. What was supposed to be one thing seemed to respond to another.

For a moment, she thought of texting Andrea, but she deleted the message before sending it. Captivated, she spent a couple hours analyzing the data. When it was very late, she set her alarm, switched off the light, and swallowed a sleeping pill.

⚙

PEDRO LIFTED HIS HEAD. His eyes were slow to focus on the hillsides looming up above. Nearby, two pigs sharing green apples, rooting around his naked feet. He dragged one leg closer and sat up, resting his back against the tree. The ground was mined with bottles leading in the direction of his father's voice.

"For fuck's sake, sit." The old man set a glass at the edge of the table.

The afternoon smelled of vinegar, of greenery animals had pissed on. They sat down to drink, avoided each other's eyes, attended to the sound of the wind that sliced the heads of passing birds. His father was already drunk, which irritated him.

"I saw the carts go by. The oxen all slow. The crack of the rocks under the wheels. The men looked asleep." The rotgut was tasteless in his throat. "And I saw the dead woman. The bug." Pedro pressed the glass in his fist. "Your wife who couldn't take the spray, couldn't deal with the dust, like the insect she was. A pest!" His father cackled, jutting his face closer to Pedro, who lurched across the table, tried to hit him, failed. His hands slowed and shrank and suddenly his body was the size of a chicken, and he had to take off hopping, stunned, then bury his head in the ground so the old man wouldn't make a casserole out of him.

He thought he heard María. He was sure: not her voice but some kind of warm presence traveling from far away, guiding him. It was as if the world were made of touch. A whole environment of damp earth. A bleeding gash. He pushed at the darkness that engulfed him and made his way forward as if heeding a thirst, trailing a thread of his own body in his wake. For some reason, what seemed to be inside him felt transported there from outside. There was the echo of the voice calling out to him, but his body was an ambiguous border. Pedro advanced, joining whatever he found down below, insects, corpses, roots, ground rock, and the contact expanded him, like a white shadow underground.[6]

⚙

"AS FAR AS WE KNOW," Giovanna addressed the room of academics, "*Cryptococcus neoformans* appears primarily in immunocompromised people, which makes it opportunistic, in a sense. Cases of a normal system being affected by fungi are scarce and have been documented only in British Columbia.

"In 1999, an outbreak of *Cryptococcus gattii*, a yeast species from the same family, but notably more complex and

---

6 When he heard things, it was like opening his eyes. When the thread touches the dream, another begins, where one's own self broadens and jumbles together with its surroundings. The body grows populous with images, things of memory, but also desires once harbored, the urges from beyond, and the truth is like gazing on a brand-new color.

aggressive, emerged on Vancouver Island, in Canada, where cases of infection were reported in animals and people. Which is extremely strange, since the environment constituted by a mammal's average temperature is unsustainable for most of the fungi kingdom. A considerable number of people, along with a variety of cats, dogs, raccoons, and other mammals, died of the infection.

"As I was saying, only two serotypes of this mushroom (B and C) have been described, and they adhere via the inhalation of propagules released into the atmosphere: a kind of lethal blight that's ingested into the body, then wreaks havoc on the lungs and nervous system. Symptoms of infection include a severe cough and shortness of breath, often accompanied by shakes, night sweats, hallucinations, random muscle spasms, cramps, hand tremors, and anorexia. Approximately ninety percent of all patients develop cryptococcal meningitis, and only two percent survive.

"One of my studies, published in a British Mycological Society journal, states that while the infection once predominantly affected elderly and chronically ill individuals, that is no longer the case today. Until 1999, all cases of C. *gattii* infections had been registered in subtropical regions, mainly in Australia, where the mushroom is endemic. However, the Vancouver outbreak marked a radical change in how we understand the fungal infection and the threat of this pathogen in particular. Indeed, this outbreak not only revealed an increase in the mortality rate of C. *gattii*—which jumped from a percentage of 0.94 cases per million inhabitants each year to 3,400 cases per million inhabitants each year—but also the mushroom's capacity to travel across continents and produce invasive outbreaks that, unless controlled, could develop into a pandemic.

"The explanation presented by the National Academy of Sciences, in the United States, involves the planet's rising temperatures due to climate change, and, especially, large-scale monoculture in areas near human communities.

"The government of Australia has shown special interest in funding research into the control and eradication of this fungus, because the tree with which C. *gattii* most frequently and effectively associates, and the only one on which its fruiting bodies reach maturity en masse, is the *Eucalyptus globulus,* endemic to Australia and commonly known as the eucalyptus.

"That said, as our country houses nearly two million hectares of eucalyptus plantations, the risk of a new outbreak is, to say the least, substantial. A single mycelium can spread up to a thousand hectares on release. Moreover, the mortality rate of this mushroom appears to be more radical. Of the five cases recently documented among forestry workers, only one is still alive: a man who spent almost two months in a coma and has, miraculously, awakened."

PART TWO

PEDRO THE VAST

Because I did feel, that is why I speak to you now as myself. I was vast once, I was not merely. I was not I when I felt people place their feet on us. I saw squads of dogs and men jacketed in blue, letters on white garments with eyes attentive to the trees, to the thickets, they never focused deeper down. Hello, I said to them, I wished to, but I didn't speak: I was no longer separate. I felt them pass, not hurting, yet they broke us. With every step we lost our hair, my large nerves split. It didn't matter, we would grow again, we knew it. There is no number that can reach us. We are always twining up from below. All together, we are so many that no name could fit around us.

Seeing you now, of course, feeling you, nothing is as it was. I break if asked to speak, it makes a separation of me. I remember this fear, the fear of my voice uttering itself, my own voice heard, a shame of air around the rest. The life that was a horse trampled over me for a long time and there I couldn't recompose myself. But I was I, do you understand? To be one and not vast is the trouble.

HOW SHOULD I TELL HER? What should I say? The weather's so weird, how long since it rained? Mom's seeing this somewhere, I know it. Do dead people know things or do they just watch? Why don't they help? Mom, I asked for Dad to wake up. What do I tell Cata now? Catita, Dad opened his eyes. He's awake. I didn't ask for his head to get fucked up.

Patricio sat in thought at the bus stop outside the hospital. He watched the circle of reporters disperse across the street, the parked white cars, the doctors telling the cameras that all updates would be suspended until further notice because the patient needed to rest. A dog wove its way through the crowd and paused by a car. It pissed against a wheel, scratched an ear, and trotted away, vanishing around the corner.

His cell phone rang as he opened the front door of the house.

"Hello?"

"Patricio? Patricio Marambio?"

"Yeah?"

"Hi, it's your Aunt Carmela. How are you?"

"My aunt, my ass."

And he hung up.

It was the tenth time someone had called wanting information about his father. They were journalists at first, professionals haranguing despite his refusals, ignorant to the blade of their questions, the searing heat they sliced in him. But that didn't last long.

Soon, other voices started calling. Pranksters, impostors, quacks. Identities forged for the sake of scrounging up any little scrap they could find. A name, some memory of his father. It went on like this until some guy had the gall to ask about his mom, about the photos of her he shared on Facebook every once in a while. Patricio proposed they talk in person. They agreed to meet up later that day, at sundown, in a park on the outskirts of the city.

The reporter was smoking outside a white van. He stared out at the playground equipment, deserted, discolored. Patricio came with backup and grabbed the guy by the neck. He and two other boys managed to shove him against a wall, kneed him in the gut a couple times, enough for him to open his mouth and end up with his recorder stuffed in it.

"Fire away, motherfucker. Ask anything you want."

At home, he turned off his phone and left it on the table. He went into the kitchen, fed the cats, and set a pot of water to boil. It was almost five and Catalina was supposed to be on her way home. He switched on his laptop. The sound of cats chewing. The water idling on the stove. The little girl staring out at the timber plantations through the window of the bus, getting sleepy on the ride. The air making room for the shrill of bubbles under pressure.

⚙

The definitions are seeds. In their grace, the essence grants us its burgeons and we know things. What I knew doesn't come from what was seen and folded into oneself. Smooth essences, noble faces, uncarved, descend if we're able to prepare, if we open ourselves to the great nerve, if we listen underneath. Their voice defines the seed, it breathes slowly and brings truth. Whoever hears it has a forest inside. The cloth tears. Its word enacts the genesis of what it says.

⚙

NO ONE UNDERSTOOD anything at first. The doctor diagnosed him with a fleeting psychotic break as a consequence of the coma, but as the days passed, some of the nurses detected another complexity. A strange angel had seized control of his face. When Patricio went to see him, his words had already lost their connection to the world, and his contaminated body seemed to have no trace of its former self. This expanded the halo of shame and confusion around Patricio. He couldn't stand it. Shaking off a nurse's arm, he stormed out weeping, wondering whether it was a sin to think that death might have been more comfortable for him. It was then, as Patricio walked home, that the first man of faith appeared at Pedro's side.

His name was Balthasar. He'd gone to the hospital to visit his grandmother as she recovered from a broken hip: Her dog Sweet Tooth, which she called Sweetie, had caught her by surprise one morning by skittering up the wooden stairs that connected the small living room to the upstairs bedroom. She couldn't dodge him in time, and the old fox terrier fell too, both rolling about in a jumble of yelps and fractures that no one else knew a thing about until after five, when she finally managed to sit, brace herself against an arm of the couch, and call her grandson. The dog, unfortunately, never woke up.

During the story of the fall, which she repeated like a scratched CD, a few words in the adjacent room caught the priest's attention. Balthasar got up and left the room, letting his grandmother's listless hand lie slack on the blanket. Standing in the hall, he pricked his ear and heard:

The circle that exists in nature and the idea of the existing circle are both in God and both the selfsame thing.

Balthasar addressed a nurse who was chatting in the hall. She sensed his curiosity.[7]

---

7 Of course Cristina would lend a hand; she'd always identified more with her faith than with her profession, never missed a Sunday mass. When Balthasar requested time alone with Pedro, she never hesitated to help. Didn't even get paid for it. A single word from the priest sufficed: She longed to serve, desperately sought to live a life of good deeds, after years of guilt that kept her up at night. In that hospital, the head nurse could pull more strings than any doctor. It wasn't hard to get someone out of there.

"It's a strange case, you know?" she confessed. "The gentleman spent two months in a coma and now that he's awake, we can't seem to shut him up."

🔆

People are free to make mistakes. Intolerance—sundering, inquisitive—doesn't understand. One is lost, spinning in circles, his blood boils, it's all a muddle when the time comes to choose. If one must sin, then let him sin while thinking of God. You are the sin. I am the sin. But if we returned to our place among the muchness, all and both in myriads, in what we once were, then no sin could be committed, nor coldness, nor sundering lies. What mistake does water make in coursing down the falls? In what muddle is the tree enmeshed when it pitches backward onto the ground? If vast, we would be a joyful well. A mode immense, a spilled silhouette.

🔆

AFTER BALTHASAR CAME the faithful: a flock of purple tunics that took over visiting hours. Kind, they befriended the nurses, gifted eucalyptus candy and prayer books to anyone casting the evil eye around the second-floor waiting room.

It was a curious congregation that claimed Pedro as its prophet. In several prior cults, Balthasar had told the "collegians,"[8] as they called themselves, that after the two biblical

---

8   While the creed had been part of the evangelical church of Curanilahue for several years, the turn of the millennium had witnessed its conversion to another doctrine, which its members called the Collegiate.

falls—Adam in Eden and Jesus on the Cross—a third messiah was expected to arrive, one who would bring about the resurgence of the Word and the kingdom of freedom on Earth. Compelled by this conviction, when Balthasar was sure that the proper individual had been identified, they rechristened him Pedro "the Vast,"[9] then surrounded him and made it impossible for Patricio's visits to continue. The door to the room stayed shut, despite Patricio's insistence. The nurses said his father's condition had declined, he'd suffered internal bleeding, better come back tomorrow. And tomorrow it was the same story all over. But Patricio, red with rage, listened from the hall as a low voice raved inside the room. After several weeks, he made one final attempt, only to be refused entry yet again. He ended up cursing everyone, shoving nurses and collegians alike, and resolved that he and his sister would never go back, his father was crazy, as he dragged Cata by the hand, leading her far away from the hospital.

Every afternoon during this period, Balthasar, leader of the congregation, devoted himself to transcribing Pedro's "sermons." He did so in a notebook, writing by hand, in a process as tedious as it was imperative, for he believed that

---

This fused Mennonite Anabaptism with the peculiar ideas of Don Décimo Contreras, the Church's founding father, and then those of Balthasar, a self-taught Latinist and rationalist.

9 *Vast* said the murmur and the disciples settled there like weeds straining for sun on a felled log. Few knew how to heed his injured word. Many were eager for the secret, as one sustaining a vessel in his hands while walking, and from head to head they shredded it and replaced it with words that induce separation. Business of rites, seed of contagion.

the speech was only real when heard directly in his voice.[10] Said notes would lay the groundwork for *The Compendium of Pedro the Vast,* tenets of the faith that the collegians propagated around a man once heard solely by his children. Sort of a shifty guy, as Juan Carlos confessed to a journalist from the *Concepción Star:* You could never be sure what he was thinking. He had a strange, dark sense of humor that had taken a turn for the worse after his wife's death.

One thing was certain: The Pedro who emerged from his coma was a different Pedro altogether. The collegians said that his words yielded comprehension, "divine ecstasy." And through the city spread the rumor of a miraculous Christ with a river's thunderous voice that touched anyone listening with its mercy. The speculation swelled on the day Dr. Moreno discharged him, and the prophet, instead of returning home, was taken to the collegians' church about a mile outside Curanilahue.

The Door, as they called it, was a modest compound of wooden houses inhabited by most of the community. The site once belonged to a tire repair shop that had sold it to them for cheap in the early 2000s. There God revealed the spot where the church was supposed to sit. And the first brothers

---

10 There was no spiritual premise for it: Pedro's dictation occasionally took the form of a babble, tight and hoarse as a swarm, from which it was difficult to extract any logical meaning. As a result, it may be that the *Compendium* contained more of Balthasar's imagination than of Pedro's own voice.

and sisters arrived, following Balthasar, laboring for several years to build a chapel and a humble housing complex they ringed with a eucalyptus grove that by the time Pedro arrived had grown into mature trees, lending shade and a cool vigor to the whole place.

After he was set up in the cabin where the priest lived, no one looked Pedro in the eye, addressed him directly, or saw him at all, except on Sundays. Balthasar and several trusted collegians were responsible for taking care of him, dressing him, feeding him, and preparing him for his spiritual sermons.

·☼·

HE FILLED THE KETTLE. The water was dark and you had to boil it before drinking. He used a lighter to start two burners, placing the pot on one and a pan to heat rolls on the other. He took his cell phone out of his pocket. Catalina was lying on the couch in her parka, eyes fixed on her own phone. Light flickered across her face. Patricio had told her she'd have to go to bed after her snack, since it was already late and there was no way to heat the living room. Stubborn, she pulled the neck of her parka up over her mouth and nestled deeper into the cushions.

They were both more interested in the news they found online than in the broadcast on the old TV set, sitting dormant under an embroidered cloth across the room, crowned with a cactus, switched on by force of habit alone. Patricio

watched a video of the tornado assailing the village of Los
Ángeles. Astonished, he called out to his sister. When she
didn't answer, he went and sat down beside her on the couch.

"Look."

"What?" Catalina didn't glance up from her own screen.

The video had been shot from a gas station and showed a
roiling sky, apocalyptically gray. Trash floated in it, clothes,
trees, debris hurled in centrifugal orbits among wild sparks
from high-tension cables, cars skittering like plastic cups.
People sought refuge wherever they could. A violent cloud
veered toward a little town, and the roofs threatened to
fly clean off. Patricio watched, fascinated, as if it were a
science-fiction movie, but his sister didn't seem to care, not
even when this was all happening a hundred miles from home.

"Hungry," she said, with her nose still stuck under the
neck of her coat. "I'm hungry!" she repeated, then dropped
the phone and flopped onto her belly, leaning over the tiles to
draw, tapping her toes together.

She was going to catch a cold, Patricio thought. She'd better get up, it was time for bed, but she looked so focused that
he decided to leave her be. He heard the scratch of her marker
on the page, the tip so dry it barely worked, and got up to finish preparing their snack. The smell of toast made him think
back to a time of more exacting seasons, not this mishmash
of winter and summer, the cynical forecast of their present.
In the morning, he'd leave the house with three layers on and
strip down to his T-shirt by noon, clutching the others in his

hand. But at night a damp cold rose up from the unheated floor, forcing them to sleep, dangerously, with the fire lit, and then he wondered if the world was careening straight toward its end, if the gray clouds churning in the distance weren't the horsemen of hunger and death, galloping in circles, slashing the rain, as he picked up the bread and touched the black space in the burnt roll until an electric impulse fused the burn and the pleasure of lifting the smarting fingertip to his mouth.

He set a mug and the buttered bread on the floor beside his sister and reached out to stroke her hair. She hummed a reggaeton song as she blew on the eucalyptus tea. Some time back, he'd adopted the habit of infusing the same leaves as the ones Pedro boiled to clear his lungs. This tree also supplied their firewood: Patricio would cut the lower limbs at night, when he imagined the guards at the neighboring tree plantation were done with their rounds, sweat-soaked as he crossed the electric fence.

He acted the part of the grownup. He made sure that Catalina kept going to school and that the house had the basics for them to keep living there. His sister, though, ignored his zeal to provide, taking him no more seriously than if they were playing house. She knew nothing had changed. That very afternoon, she'd said, You're not the dad, you can't tell me what to do, then slammed her bedroom door. And he'd stood there, staring after her, furious and ashamed. Later, vengeful, as Catalina sat up for a sip of tea, he plopped down at her side, grabbed a marker, and started to cover her

drawing with scribbles and eyebrows and slashes and whis-
kers, scrawling over the characters and circles and straight
lines still peeking from the corners of the paper. Catalina let
out a shriek of rage. She leapt to her feet and stabbed the
green marker into Patricio's cheek, snuffing his red laughter.
Stamping her foot, she stormed off to her room and slammed
the door again.

Patricio rubbed his cheek and studied the drawing, sullen.
In the middle of the paper, a little girl pointed at a fire. On
the far right, a tornado pierced the sky. On the other side, a
mushroom-shaped cloud concealed a conversation between
two men in the woods. At the bottom of the drawing was the
figure of a boy, crying, pants down, holding a lightning bolt
in his hand.

⚙

SHE THOUGHT ABOUT the desire of mushrooms, the impulse
born as a single stain, then expanding for miles. Does it ever
hold itself back, hesitate to go on? Giovanna wondered, blowing on a cup of chamomile tea. She was deep in her reading.
Transported, given over to it. Day by day, different interpre-
tations of the data multiplied on her desk. Maybe fungi are
too intelligent to doubt: It would be an irresponsible expen-
diture of energy, she thought. Who does it answer to, the
thread of body, the white speck growing in all directions,
trawling millions of spores into the light?

A thin transparent film coated the mushrooms. Giovanna

set them onto the cutting board next to the minced garlic and chucked the plastic tray. She was in the final stretch of writing a book about the symbiosis of certain infectious lichens and trying to stabilize her routine, deliver regular installments to her publishing house. Cook, read, sleep. Open her eyes and check the time in a panic. Accelerate her body as it awaited some slow synapse to translate for her. Rub her eyes with her fist. Scrub the dishes. Sleep again.

The days passed as if in quarantine. Her workspace sometimes changed, the sheets, the ideas shaping more excuses than theories.

"No going out until the chapter is done," she promised herself with the rigor of a religious mandate. "No checking your phone."

Then she'd go to the bathroom and examine the cracks at the corners of her lips, like tiny mouths sprouting from her own. It was as if the fungus wanted to tell her something. Was there room for a sign on her open skin? For a vowel? Her eyes dried out and her mind occasionally thought on its own. She felt her ocular muscle attentive to the trails of her sentences, while another section, thicker, its own boss, took a walk around the park, dug a hole with its hands, got covered in dirt.

She thought about the face of the man who'd woken up. Pale skin tight against the bone. She'd seen something similar in patients with acute fungal infections: their bodies, when they finally vanquished the invading pathogen, were left so depleted that they soon died from some unrelated affliction. A cold, for example. But how can such a widespread presence be so abruptly eliminated? The image explained that the fungus had entered through the meninges. It was as if it had decided to make a sudden exit of its own accord. A mere feat of the immune system? Couldn't there be a symbiotic relationship between the two bodies? Giovanna had pledged to steer clear of such ideas.

Her phone started to vibrate from its precarious perch on the refrigerator, threatening to land among the mushrooms now in the pan. She managed to catch it before it fell.

"Hello? Yes, this is she. Yes. Look, it depends." She lowered the flame under the pan to keep the mushrooms from drying out. "What's the subject of the report, please?" She slid a bowl of rice into the microwave. "I'll have to check— Could it be next week? Great. What's the address?" She went into the bedroom, then returned to the kitchen with her free hand clutching several dirty mugs. "Okay, I'll send you the budget. Take care."

Giovanna retreated to her room and made a couple notes on the wall calendar. In her erratic handwriting: "meeting araucana timber enterprises."

☼

THE CATS WERE sick. Catalina sat on the floor outside the kitchen and snapped her fingers. Three weary animals approached when they heard the sound. She set down a dish of warm milk with two Tylenols dissolved in it. The gaunt cats lapped slowly as she stroked their heads.

Her brother watched from the living room couch, where he'd flopped in front of the TV. For a moment, he remembered how his friend Enzo used to put out cans of tuna mixed with crushed glass for the alley cats. They'd both been young, newly interested in the world. You ever think about dying, Enzo had said as he steadily ground the glass in a mortar. I bet it's like when the power goes out, Patricio replied, staring at the piece of macerated windowpane, recalling the time his father asked if he knew what glass was made of, seconds before tossing a fistful of sand in his face. Patricio felt the skinny cats compressing their yowls as Enzo rapped a finger against the lid of the tuna can, peeled it open, and mixed everything with a spoon. He pictured lampposts, life traveling through cables, overhead wires, the cough of a creature poisoned by a belly grenade. His friend told him to watch the eyes of the dying cats, wait for their pupils to widen, for the moment when the blackness makes a fog of the air. Spasm, cut, and the blood lightens.

He got up from the couch and walked to the door. The cats drank laboriously, tremors passing through their desolate bodies, ribs stark as if trying to shed the skin. Patricio knew they were going to die. He opened the cabinet and took out one of the three remaining cans of tuna. He told his sister to move aside and emptied the can into the milk. The cats lifted their heads. Their pupils looked like the lenses in a pair of shattered eyeglasses. Patricio felt a line of cool sweat trickle down his back, remembered his father's shouts and blows a few months prior, thick hands gripping the collar of his shirt, lifting him against the wall. It was all because of a taunt. The blind gaze, the sharp laugh, distended around him like a fence in the middle of the soccer game, that "I'm gonna fuck your dead mom, Marambio," before the red, before Enzo saying life needs a knife to the throat, and Patricio taking his word for it: He grabbed his friend by the neck, threw him to the ground, and smashed his head until the world narrowed into white smoke, face hidden then, between the pillow and the mattress, talking to his mother, drool streaming from the corner of his mouth, the voice, the sheet, her listening, answering in his head, stroking him like a cat that comes to perch on his shoulders, like the sound of wind in the pines or the breathing of a solitary teenager in the yard. The world is free in the middle of the day, an ocean of land to cry in, head bowed, the dark of the damp room in summer, the noon heat and his uniform, the pause hung like the taste of dry dirt in the throat, the black water, dense metals in the body, sparks, twitches, bottles scattering into a brick wall, flat sobs, the light that calls him home, to stay put for a long time, to sleep and think.

"All right, let them eat," he told his sister.

"Are they going to be okay?"

They went into the house. They shut the door and sat in front of the TV. Night soon fell, and when Patricio got up to put the kettle on, the power cut.

He looked at his sister in the dark.

"Come on, Cata," he said. "Let's go to bed."

·¤·

Everything, once it is there, endeavors to keep being. In nature, nothing comes about without something stronger to destroy it. Does the moth sob, does the toad sob when the heron plucks it? Any world will dangle from a thread shuddered by wind. Just as death defeats life and consumes it, so too must there be life to swallow death.

·¤·

DURING HER PHD, Giovanna would spend entire days gathering mushrooms. This was what she loved most: snapping polypores and mycelium threads all afternoon, then taking them to the lab for analysis. There were many purposes for the interpretation of these beings: to formally study the hyphae of fast-growing mushrooms, so as to evaluate their capacity for artificial propagation; to precisely measure, grid by grid, a single *Armillaria ostoyae,* which could measure nearly two square kilometers underground; or to examine the symbiosis of different kinds of infectious lichen. Of course, some of her walks had other objectives. Every once in a while, she still remembered a visit to the Blackley Nature Preserve, where she'd sprawled in the grass with Tiffany, having ingested one *Amanita muscaria* each, and surrendered to a caress that moved softly from her neck to the edge of her ear, recognizing a sense of fellowship between each strand of hair, blade of grass, and thought, a single desire blowing the damp breeze over the afternoon, watching the clouds pass to the rhythm of her eyelids, and later the paranoia, breathing heavily, hemmed in by a forest of hazelnut trees that swelled with every step.

Giovanna looked up and a flock of pigeons flew past the window. The truth is, although she'd spent weeks reviewing the preparations for her trip every night, there was always something left to do. Along with her book, this expedition was her chief priority and concern: bringing several colleagues from England to the ends of the earth called for serious calculations. Now she wasn't sure if the car would be ready. She searched WhatsApp for Señora Marta's number. How's everything going? she texted, adding a snowflake emoji. Good, honey, the van will be out of the shop next week, lots of rain here but the sun's coming out soon, don't worry, my husband knows the road. Giovanna smiled with real excitement and sent a thumbs-up to the other end of the country.

An hour later, waiting at a traffic light, she watched people entering the regional hospital of Concepción. A small, lucky number that indicated a sensible mortality margin, now that the risk of a cryptococcosis epidemic in the area had been ruled out. The red light let her focus on what was most important. Calculate the costs of the research trip, picture the journey by van, traveling with seven specialists from the university where she'd landed as a mere third world student.

Green light. Leaving the city, Giovanna played at counting the soldiers posted outside the banks, the gas stations,
the malls that ceded to hillsides of trees, felled and soon to
be felled, protagonists of a middling, barren landscape. She
stared out the windshield on her way to visit the site of the
first infection.

That day, she was met by two executives from Araucana
Timber Enterprises: a risk management officer and the foreman at Plant H. The company had hired her as a consul-
tant in drafting the fatality report for the four other infected
workers. Diligent in their way, the executives ushered her into
an office at the back of the enormous gleaming glass ware-
houses, where they presented her with printed studies of the
plantation and soil, the same ones she'd already received and
reviewed by email.

The risk management officer, a short, hair-gelled man
in a red tie, asked her to take a seat at the desk where his
computer was, then turned the screen for them both to see.
Giovanna's eyes followed the cursor to the folder with the
report on the previous six-month period. The man lowered
the cursor until it reached the report he needed. The titles of
the files followed a repetitive formula:

worker dies caught in wood chipper worker dies in
vehicular accident worker suffers traumatic amputation fingers left hand while cutting wood with cross-
cut saw worker dies caught in equipment blade worker

fatally intoxicated by drinking liquid pesticide worker suffers traumatic amputation of right thumb in pto shaft worker suffers traumatic amputation index finger while detaching wood caught in circular saw worker dies of allergic reaction to fungicide worker suffers traumatic injury of right middle finger stacking wood worker suffers traumatic injury of distal phalanx of ring finger in pellet machine worker suffers contamination from aerial spraying of pesticide worker suffers traumatic amputation of pinky finger on contact with teeth of milling machine worker dies crushed by moving parts of machinery worker falls from roof of warehouse when fiber sheet breaks worker suffers fatal accident while operating band saw in sawmill worker dies caught in bark shredder

"Here it is: May three," said the risk management officer, the cursor hovering on the file he'd sought.

Impatient, Giovanna rubbed her right hand, cracked her knuckles. She wondered how twelve years of studies hadn't gotten her any further than a consulting gig. The stamp of a specialist. Explaining, signing, submitting her invoice. In truth, neither doctors nor businessmen seemed to take her very seriously. A software program could have done this, she thought. All it took was a database.

The risk management officer finished outlining the deaths of Omar Tralcal, age forty, Calixto Morales, thirty-three,

Gerardo Huenante, twenty-nine, and Alexis Fernández, twenty-six, who had a shared wake the month prior; the funeral was organized by the Confederation of Forestry Workers. Then he asked Giovanna to corroborate the data related to the infection. She leaned closer to the screen, carefully read the five lines, and pointed out an error in the spelling of "cryptococcosis."

Now that the report was ready, the case was filed and the probability of new infections in Plant H duly dismissed. For an instant, on her way out, Giovanna registered a peculiar sense of guilt. She wondered if the other infected worker, the one who'd woken up, was still alive.

An armored vehicle waited outside the company. Three young men in monotone uniforms, assault weapons resting by their boots, chewed gum and stared as she passed. The risk management officer shook her hand and went back into the office. Before she got back in her car, Giovanna looked up and admired the sky: a spectacle of magnificent, incendiary clouds. She took her cell phone out of her pocket. Snapped a photo.

ON WEEKEND AFTERNOONS when he was young, Balthasar would leave the bakery and make his way to church, where he'd throw himself into studying Latin grammar in a back room. He'd open the heavy book and rest it on the table, which sat under a painting with the expression *nihil volentibus*

arduum[11] etched in bronze. He'd read meticulously, as if the person who'd given him the book was the person who'd written it, each word suffused with their affection. Patient, he'd convey the verbs to their cases and declinations: an artisanal labor he liked comparing to the construction of a watch or a drawbridge.

"Very good, my child. That's enough." Balthasar looked up at the sound of Reverend Contreras's voice. The light streamed in with its timid kinsfolk of dust, entering the room through a tall, narrow window that only dimly lit his reading. "There's no use in pressing on like this."

Dusk was falling, and the father didn't think it wise to force his vision against the text. Reading poorly due to exhaustion causes long-term damage, he often said. We mustn't wear out our eyes. Balthasar closed the book and picked up his backpack. His teacher walked him to the door.

"How do you feel?"

"B-b-b-better, Father," Balthasar replied, turning his head. His bent neck and stooped shoulders gave him the air of a weary tree.

The father stopped. "Listen, son, are you cold?"

Balthasar shook his head.

"Are you ashamed?"

"It's n-n-not that, F-father."

As hard as he tried to hide it, his stutter always made its

---

11 "Nothing is impossible for the willing."

presence known. The words would catch against the roof of his mouth and come out all stuck together as his classmates mimicked him, waving their hands and scrawling "Balthasasasasar" in his notebook. A doctor attributed the problem to his mother's job as a temporary farm worker during her pregnancy. Pesticide exposure doesn't just harm the mother, it also causes learning disabilities in her child, the doctor explained in a hoarse, distant voice. Meanwhile, Balthasar stared at the wall as if tracking flies, and his grandmother, irritated, sat through the speech about "special education" yet again.

The reverend placed a hand on his shoulder and continued. "So you aren't feeling any sorrow? Or rage? It's good to acknowledge our negative passions, child." Balthasar looked down at the reverend's feet. "You'll see: People think we're split into two kinds of affections. But our nature is far more complex." Together, they stepped out of the dingy little room and took their coats and scarves. The chapel's warm air felt good to Balthasar, helped him straighten up and listen better to the priest, whose figure, lit by the fluorescent tubes, glanced off the paintings and crosses all around them. "He who finds good only when the circumstances bring him closer to himself will find nothing in evil but helplessness. And so, from one side of the scale to the next, he will advance irresolutely through life, rising and falling, growing ever more fearful of the day when he cannot get to his feet." The reverend stopped at the threshold of the metal door, didn't open it, and kept speaking, his back to the boy. "Nature is God, Balthasar, and it is one and the same for everyone. Without Him, we move blindly through the world. Only He can direct our eyes ahead of us so that we may understand the order exceeding and determining us at every instant. On Judgment Day, no matter what we believe, all of God's creatures will turn to His word. Wretched and fortunate alike, we will rise from the ground and from the water and listen to the dictates of truth."

Balthasar couldn't hold back his tears. He thought of his father punching his mother against a wall. Rage like glass scraping inside his bones. He tried to connect what the reverend was saying with his own story, and then came air, a loosening of his tongue's superior longitudinal muscle; then the sweet thread springing from his eyes. Balthasar looked at the old man, who smiled with great enthusiasm, and thought of his grandmother. Contreras opened the door and a frigid wind gusted in. Young Balthasar straightened his back, wiped his tears, and stepped out.

Coiling his scarf around his neck, Balthasar admired the wind that blustered dry leaves onto the priest, scattered them onto his coat, his cheeks, his dense eyebrows, then restored them to the air, where they floated down onto the concrete. Contreras tucked the church keys in his coat pocket and spoke again.

"Balthasar, I'd like you to go home tonight and think about your father. I'd like you to acknowledge that he too is someone's son. Imagine that his progenitor is also within you and try to forgive him. And his father before him, and before that father, the previous, and so on, until you get all the way back to Christ, all the way up to God. I want you to learn to see how the past speaks for us, how it folds and changes against us."

The reverend shook his hand goodbye. Balthasar felt the chill of his wizened skin, which stayed with him as he crossed the street. Later, sitting at the bus stop, he watched two ulmo trees crisscrossing their branches, as if sheltering each other, and sank his hands deep into his armpits, pressing into his body.

ON HER WAY home, she drove right into a demonstration. Anxiety simmering, Giovanna slid the car around the protesters and barricades, gesturing apologetically, doors locked, distrusting the distance between the flames and the tires, the unpredictability of the crowd, although they seemed to be focused on the special forces approaching simultaneously from the coast and from the north of the city with a lacerating smell that forced everyone to cover their noses with whatever they had on hand. Desperate, Giovanna yelled and honked until she found an opening to accelerate through, just as the cops began to shoot, right at torso level, at the people who'd taken to the streets early in the day—and who were trying to answer the pellets and tear gas fired at their bodies with adjectives and hunks of cement.

Giovanna, sweating, shut her apartment door, set down the boxes by the washing machine, and collapsed on the couch, making a strange, clumsily calculated gesture to peel off her purse without releasing her phone. The line was busy. She texted Andrea that she'd pulled it off, she'd bought the tents: Every item on the prep list was crossed out. She checked the news. Not much had changed. A video recounted the discovery of an eight-year-old boy hanged on the outskirts of Vilcún. His family had spent the past week searching for him and the missing person campaign had spread across social media. She'd seen it in the Instagram stories of several friends, and although everyone expected the worst, the confirmation still came as a shock.

She opened the curtains. There wasn't much to see outside, but she heard noise in the distance. Ambulances, explosions, intermittent sounds, like when a refrigerator activates at random in the middle of the night. After dinner, she told Richard, her lab director in Manchester, that all the travel equipment was ready and two months was more than enough time for everyone to buy reasonable plane tickets. Then she sat down with a book by a Colombian forensic mycologist she was supposed to have finished reviewing several weeks ago. But before long, blowing into a cup of green tea, she was engrossed in reading about how Martín Millacura had dark brown eyes, how he'd been wearing a Spider-Man backpack that was found filled with rocks, how his sneakers seemed to have been put on by force, how blood and traces of urine and fecal matter were found in his underwear, how his backpack straps were stuck to the skin of his neck, how his father had been arrested recently, charged with trying to burn down a police station in Padre Las Casas, how his mother had chained herself to the local courthouse and the general director of the police force had sent his condolences to the family.

Giovanna shared the article on Twitter with the hashtag *#justiceformartin* and checked her email. The latest issue of the *Mycology Journal* from Austral University included an article on new lichen in Punta Curiñanco Park; her surname and Andrea's appeared as coauthors. Giovanna shared the paper with her, smiling to herself, and then the lights in the apartment flickered. Startled, she stood in the middle of the living room, wondering for an instant if she should call Andrea again. Then she refocused on the screen. She was surprised to discover a few typos and extra spaces in the published text. She hoped she was the only person reading it. Longed for the website to randomly crash, keeping the article hidden. Not available. Page under construction.

☼

IT WAS MIDMORNING when Patricio went into the yard. The sun took its time to burn off the brusque fog seeping into the corners. He stretched out his foot between some flowerpots and managed to extract a ball with one swift jerk; it rolled toward him, eager as a puppy. The material showed its age:

The stamp of the number 90 surfaced like a once-beautiful face, its gold faded against the scratched solid white of the leather. Patricio tossed it into the air and kept it afloat, bumping it on his insole, coaxing his mind to linger on every touch, to let itself be carried along by this soft, exacting bounce against his body.

It cheered him, this form of concentration. The pain rarely eased. His father once said doing Sudoku puzzles made him feel something like that. It's like there's this white smoke around your vision, Pedro told him, you barely notice it, but it's there: focusing on what you have in front of you, erasing any excess that disrupts your attention.

Patricio wondered whether people might feel too much. He looked at the kittens splayed beside their mother, a dog napping in the sun. Maybe there's something wrong with humans, he thought. A species error that makes it too hard for us to live alone. He felt it sometimes when he smoked with his friends and briefly doubted that his hands were his. What if they were being controlled by a spirit or a gust of spores that had gotten into his head. And so what if he himself were nothing but an illegitimate echo, the unconscious repetition of someone else's words? Occasionally he'd express these things to his friends and they'd howl with laughter. Sick weed, huh, they'd say. Pass the joint, you're talking like your daddy. And he'd laugh too. His humor was different from his father's. Maybe the species gradually improved and each generation was kinder than the previous. It wasn't impossible.

But his sister seemed to disprove the theory. Sometimes he'd catch her chasing mice around the yard, setting makeshift traps, bringing them to the kittens as a gift. Other times he'd hear her laughing silently to herself as she watched shipwrecked insects and leeches that she'd caught in bottles, inspecting them with the flashlight of her cell phone. Once, after he'd scolded her for giving Butter a lizard as a present, he wondered if what his sister did with animals was truly bad. All living things eat each other, he thought later, joint in hand, taking his time before passing it, in those seconds that felt like the eternal bounce of a ball against his foot. Was this thinking, really? Letting yourself be this far from yourself? All living things suck at air, water, time—and what if the disease was doing the same with his father? If the whole business was just a microorganism's way of taking over a larger organ? Like the bad luck of being born a lizard and encountering a cruel little girl. Life, full stop. Acknowledging that today we get to play with a ball and tomorrow it will burst, that the river runs away from us, fires burn forests, cows shit, and that shit breeds flies and mushrooms and trees and mammals that eat each other and shit each other out, all different, all separate, all trapped in the end by the same flames.

"Hey. Hey, Pato, you gonna pass that or what?"

He dropped the ball. He watched it roll until it bumped into the empty chicken coop. He stopped short, put his hands on his hips, and looked up at the sky. A gathering of gray clouds approached. Wind blew. It turned cold for a bit, then passed. Suddenly it was hot. The weather was weird. Maybe it would rain in the afternoon, or at night. Maybe not.

·ọ·

RUMORS SPREAD THROUGH the congregation that the prophet's condition was getting worse. A strange sickness was hewing wounds in his skin and emitted a terrible smell. Only Balthasar had any direct contact, feeding him nothing but dense oatmeal with boiled apples and bathing him with lengths of delicate satin cloth. He asked Pedro not to speak much as he washed his feet, to save his voice for important matters. The sermons, meanwhile, were in fine shape. The congregation grew more profitable; before long, the number of devotees—and *Compendium* sales—was overwhelming. Lately, Pedro's sermons all but filled the parish.

There, the young priest and community leader saw no contradiction with the precepts of his doctrine, which were condensed into five basic shared rules.[12] Still, his mentor was less

---

12   Thus did *The Compendium of Pedro the Vast* set forth its "rules for the proper guidance of collegians":

I. Speak in a manner intelligible to the multitude, so as to produce a common language. The benchmark for this tongue is Pedro's own.

II. Indulge ourselves with pleasures only insofar as they are necessary for preserving health.

III. Obtain only sufficient money to enable the community to preserve our life and health.

IV. Follow such general customs as are consistent with our purpose, in spite of those who may oppose them.

V. Detach, to the extent possible, from all individual references in favor of communal ones.

than pleased. Periodically, with his characteristic prudence, Father Contreras would remind Balthasar that faith was not an instrument of speculation. But the once-obsequious disciple received his words with growing indifference, and the rift between them widened.

On the day the community helped him build the Door, Balthasar Sánchez's life changed forever. He had been raised by his grandmother, who'd protected him from an alcoholic stalker of a father, obsessed with regaining custody of Balthasar upon his release from prison. The man was insistent. He'd leave strange gifts, toys appearing on their doorstep overnight. He'd call at all hours, wait for him after school in defiance of the restraining order. Balthasar's grandmother would hide the boy from view, lock the door, lace a rosary around his wrist, and send him to his room, terrified that the emergency line would be busy.

One evening, as a young man, Balthasar left the bakery on Calle Cruz where he worked. He sat outside the shop to wait for the bus, eyes on the ground, thoughts stacked like fish slipping in and out of a basket as winter's rawness pierced his head. Suddenly, he noticed a group of people gathered outside a warehouse. They were all neatly dressed. They seemed cheerful, hugging each other and offering well wishes, festive as a family. In the crowd, an elderly man with a hunched back, smiling ear to ear, saw Balthasar watching and crossed the street in his direction. The young man shook with nerves, glanced back and forth to see if the bus was coming, but it was too late. The old man was already at his side, smiling. The next week, Balthasar knocked on the metal door of the congregation as he coughed and rubbed his hands for warmth. He pressed his tongue to the wall of his teeth, shifted it from hard palate to soft, tried to ignore it, leave it for dead.

Soon after the invitation to his church, Don Décimo Contreras took Balthasar as his personal disciple. Their connection was immediate. The young man didn't need to say much, as the old one was satisfied if he listened and did what he asked. In this Balthasar excelled. Over time, the reverend patiently versed him in a broad array of arts. His pupil improved, gained in personality and self-confidence. He woke early, always arrived on time to his classes and his job on weekends, then left for church. He never missed a Mass. Never left a homework assignment incomplete. Wasn't sure if he'd begun to stutter less, or if the bullying had diminished. But at least he could busy his mind with other things. Before long he was made choral director. His tongue rarely slipped when he sang his praise or repeated a prayer. Reverend Contreras loaned him books, had him participate in Mass, taught him to translate.

Now, though, Balthasar was the reverend, and he had a different problem.

One Sunday, just before sundown, old Contreras counseled his disciple for the last time: "You need to be prepared, son. If the prophet is sick, the people must know."

Balthasar shut a large leather-bound copy of the *Compendium* beside another one bound in wood, where he was translating the former into Latin. He thought of Pedro's feet, their flayed, fetid soles, skin riddled with sores, the cough he'd had for the past few weeks.

Reverend Contreras looked up from the bench where he sat, sought his eyes. "You must warn them of the danger."

GIOVANNA'S DOCTORAL DISSERTATION focused on the unusual scope that the *Cryptococcus gattii* outbreak had attained on Vancouver Island and explained its significance to contemporary mycology. In fact, hers was among the texts that made it possible for the cases to be treated as part of an epidemic and not as merely fortuitous events.

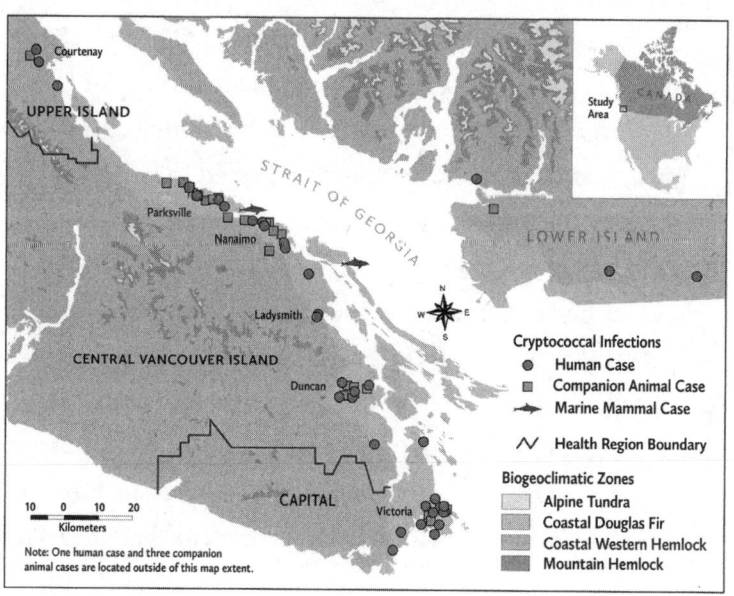

The criteria for classifying cryptococcal infection as a transmissible outbreak included the observation of symptoms consistent with cryptococcal infection and the isolation of C. *gattii* in normally sterile locations, bronchoalveolar lavages, and negative HIV states in patients. Twenty-one isolates from immunocompetent humans were included in this study. Six isolates from HIV-positive guests in BC (British Columbia), deemed unrelated to the outbreak, were included for quality control purposes. As illustrated in Figure 1, cryptococcal infection was diagnosed in 35 mammals between 2000 and 2001, including 13 dogs (*Canis familiaris*), 17 cats (*Felis catus*), two ferrets (*Mustela putorius furo*), and three Dall's porpoises (*Phocoenoides dalli*).

Thirty-five of the 38 human cases (92.1%) and 28 of the 35 animal cases (80%) were identified on the east coast of Vancouver Island. The remaining cases pertained to people who had only passed through the place. None survived (Oddó 2015, 85–86).

One of her hypotheses—which had landed her in trouble with several members of the evaluating committee—pointed to a certain peculiarity in the genetic composition of *C. gattii*. According to Giovanna, the VGII/AFLP6 genotype, recognized as the transmitter of cryptococcus in humans, demonstrated a similar assimilation process to that of certain

Cordyceps mushrooms, by entering the bodies of smaller organisms such as ants, moths, and beetles.

In the future, Giovanna explained, the mushroom might become capable of not only producing, on the basis of this genotype, "the condition affiliated with the bronchopulmonary system we generally know as cryptococcus...but also setting off a process of symbiosis with the host organism."

As Giovanna noted, such a union was most likely to occur in the central nervous system, specifically in the posterior lobe of the cerebellum. This would have consequences like those associated with the case of the bullet ant, in which the Ophiocordyceps unilateralis mushroom successfully commandeered the movements of certain members of the colony, altering their behavior to transform them into living spore sacs—which, in due time, would burst inside the anthill.

All of this, Giovanna warned, was difficult to predict in humans, considering the enormous differences in size and temperature. But given the mushroom's evolution and characteristics during the Vancouver outbreak, the possibility couldn't be ruled out. In this respect, she stated:

> Although the notion of fungal control over a person may seem like something out of science fiction and thrillers, the evidence points to an interesting consideration. In the case of people and mammals infected during this particular epidemic, the host specimen is a species of lichen—a combination of C. gattii with

the newly cataloged *Cordyceps humana*—whose communion occurs, indeed, in the cerebral cortex of the infected individuals (Oddó 2015, 180).[13]

☼

A CAT MEOWED. He could hear where it was. Patricio poked his head into the yard: nothing. Dust, winter sun. Catalina darted past him, yelling, Butter! Blanket! then stood in the doorway, summoning the air with whistles and applause. He looked at the back of his sister's neck, skin coated with grime like rust on metal. Inside, the house was losing weight, its objects sapped of substance. It was colder now. Hard to get

---

13   Although she knew nothing about it at the time, her dissertation partly foretold what came to pass at the Door, where nature began to behave very strangely. Several firefighters who arrived on the scene described a white cloud drifting through the air, affixing itself to everything it touched and producing states of altered consciousness in anyone exposed to it. It was a common symptom: A person's body was transported to the place where their eyes alighted. "I looked at a tree branch and suddenly I was all the way up in the eucalyptus, but when I tried to come down I already found myself standing on the roof of one of the white houses. I quickly ended up on the ground and there I covered my eyes with my hands, shouting for help until a comrade grabbed me by the shoulders and shook me out of it." "I thought I was a cat, I swear, the charred cat looked me in the eye and then I wasn't . . . how can I put it . . . here. In what I'm made of, you know? As if I were suddenly moving around inside the cat, with the cat, its body, its pain and mine. Mine too, you know? My very own body." "I was in a lobster-shaped cloud. That's where I got to when I saw it. All of a sudden there was the city down below, the whole thing, like the view from a plane. I thought I'd died and turned into a bird. But then I looked down at the river and that's where they fished me out, holding on to a branch, talking to myself."

up in the morning. The plumbing had run dry and the siblings had simply stopped showering.

He scratched an armpit. "Leave it alone. Are you hungry?"

Catalina knelt and pressed her hands together at her forehead. She prayed softly enough to show she was speaking to herself, but not so low that Pato couldn't hear. She was praying for the cats. She appealed to the virgin as her mother had taught her. He felt ashamed by the scene; his sister's eccentricities always made him nervous. On the last vacation they took together when María was still alive, she hadn't wanted to swim in Lleulleu Lake because she said there was a monster in it. The water is a monster, she explained. All the water on the planet is its hair.

Then she should go up to the lake and look into the water, he told her. She'd see that it wasn't a monster but something else. He'd pulled her halfheartedly by the arm, walking over the rocks, until Catalina reached the edge, a couple meters above the surface. Lean out, he said. What do you see? His sister strained her neck slowly, like a turtle, then laughed and waved to her reflection. That's the monster, Patricio had said, and pushed her in.

Now, as she began her animal supplication, Patricio went into the bathroom and turned the shower knob out of sheer habit. Discouraged, he returned to the yard and filled a bucket from one of the water drums they kept by the chicken coop. He set the contents of the bucket to boil in two pots and the kettle, took out an old towel and a clay serving dish, and brought them into the bathroom. When the water was bubbling, he called his sister.

"Take that off," he said.

"What?"

"Your clothes."

Cata wriggled out of her blue T-shirt, crumpled it, tossed it into a corner, tugged off her corduroy pants, stood there in her underwear. An acid smell fluttered around the room, as if looking for something. She sat down on the toilet lid. Patricio sank the towel into the hot water, wrung it out, and lifted one of her arms. The water droplets ran black on her skin.

"Hey, Pato, where do cats go when they die?"

"What do you mean, where?" As if he hadn't understood the question.

"Like do they go to heaven."

The truth was, he wanted to tell her that nothing goes anywhere. That it's like ripples in the water. Something flickers and returns. This water is the same water you saw in the lake. That monster has hair all over it. In my armpits, soon in yours. It's what makes our fingernails grow and circles form around a rock that vanishes into the depths. Death doesn't happen, squirt: We just get smaller. Cats are eaten by ants and the ants drown in the dirty water we toss into the yard. Even though nothing grows there anymore, it's got invisible lakes underneath. Voices of plants and beings that walk in all directions, that fear what's dry and watch from the corners of their houses, like slow spiders. What's big looks dead, but if you throw it into the lake, that's that. That's where the cat's pupils swim, the tears you cried making concentric circles. Bad water may make you hear dripping and voices in the dark, but you can scare it off. Some night, dig a hole, make a well, and look inside. The backs at your back will be with you, your reflection will be new. Stir the water with gravel, don't let it keep still. Infect it with dust and dirty cloth, little goose, until it loses heart. Gather grime for a while, then take a bath. You'll keep death at arm's length.

But he said nothing. He washed his sister's cheeks in silence, scrubbing until her dark skin regained its gleam.

"Okay, lean back," he said, and collected her hair and lowered it into the dish. He held it there for a few minutes, squeezing and releasing the strands, pressing out the dirt. Then he took her hands and placed the dish into them. "Stay there."

It was dusk; the house would be freezing soon. Patricio shut the door, walked across the living room, opened the door to the woodstove, stuck in a few dry sticks, and started a fire. Intermittent meows floated in from outside, muffled among the tree branches cut by wind. He set a few hunks of bread onto the lid and returned to the bathroom. He helped Cata dry herself with a towel she then wrapped around her head. Look, she declared, half naked, hands on her hips, swiveling the towel from side to side. I'm Mama.

Her brother smiled and asked her to come out.

"Put your PJs on, you turd. It's my turn for a bath."

Later, they sat together by the stove, sheltering in the fire's warmth that slowly dried their hair. Catalina drew and Patricio watched the embers like a TV set.

"Look, Pato," Cata said, pushing her notebook toward him. "I drew the monster."

Puzzled, he asked her which monster. It was a strange-looking stick figure, barely anthropomorphic, with a mess of arms and hands and two faces stuck to a smiling animal face.

"The presents monster. He's a good monster. He has a catfish face because he was born underwater, but one day a fisherman fished him and brought him home to live there and they made millions of pesos selling pejerrey fish and the monster wanted to give presents to the people in town and his friends from the lake, because he was nice, and he gave a bubble to his fish friend and gave a leash to his duck friend, and then he rang everybody's doorbell to make new friends, but since he was a monster people didn't want to and they didn't like him, they slammed the door in his face or threw boiling water on him, until one day the monster grabbed the fisherman and cut off his head, and he stuck the catfish face onto his face, and then he did the same thing to everyone he saw, until one night he went back into the water and decided to live down there."

The drawing seemed to move if he looked at it long enough. "And then what happened?" Patricio asked. "Did the monster die?"

"No," his sister said. "He's still alive. He sleeps in the

lake, but his lake is as big as the whole world and he can come out whenever he wants. The monster can come out in any kind of water. If you look at a puddle for a long time or a cup of tea, he can come out and eat your head off."

·ф·

ONE NIGHT, PUTTING off work on her book, Giovanna googled Araucana Timber Enterprises. Among the scores of results, she discovered one in which the firm—founded by an Italian entrepreneur who amassed a fortune during the dictatorship by selling off old public companies and lands usurped from Chilean and Mapuche peasant farmers—was currently subject to a lawsuit by the families of workers killed by cryptococcus. The article, which appeared in a local newspaper, read:

> On August 22, a group of women from Cura-nilahue presented a formal complaint to the District Attorney of Concepción over unpaid compensation from Araucana Timber Enterprises. The corporation had supposedly committed to providing financial remuneration for the death of the four forestry work-ers infected by an outbreak of contagious mushrooms at a branch of the multinational company. As stated by one of the plaintiffs, "The company promised us payment, a house, and reparations, but we haven't seen any of it. What's worse, people say things that aren't true, that we're filthy rich now, we're the *widows of.*

Sometimes people are as bad or worse than the suits, you know? They want firewood from the fallen tree. We know it's the powerful ones who put that gossip in their heads. No one around here is talking for free. Everyone's bought off. The governor himself got mad about something I said in the newspaper. What does he care what I say or think. And what about that senator, why does he get so worked up about whatever happens with the executives? But it all makes sense when you see how they treat you when you press charges. How they throw us to the pigs when we show up there at the plant, how they tear-gas our slums after we protest. We haven't gotten a single response out of them. We have no idea when the money's coming. What about my kids? Can you tell me how I'm supposed to put food on the table?" The lawsuit has yet to be processed in court. Meanwhile, Araucana Timber Enterprises has declared: "We have not delayed any monetary compensation. These complaints are baseless and ill-intentioned. It's all in the documents. The whole process has been conducted through the regular established channels. To say otherwise is slander, people lying for money. We've already done enough: a tribute to the workers at the company, sanitization of the plant under the auspices of expert consultants, and the payment of due compensation to the families."

A kind of electrical surge scaled Giovanna's back and encircled her neck, squeezed it. Did she feel guilty? For what? She only received the report, reviewed it, and did with it what any of her colleagues would have done. Besides, what did she know about these people? Why should she care about them? Wouldn't it have been more hypocritical of her to advocate for a cause in which she had no place? In any case, if she hadn't, someone else would have signed the reports, and she needed the money for the research project. Soon the firm would reopen as if nothing had happened and more trees of the same species would populate those hills and once-biodiverse forests. Workers like them, she thought, have accidents every week. In any event, it was the mushroom's fault.

·ᵜ·

THE BALL HAD DEFLATED. Patricio could only get it high enough for a mournful parabola. Frustrated, he gave it a furious kick, but it barely moved, driving up dust, less rolling than fleeing, as his kicks widened the gaps in the seams. Patricio picked up the ball and hurled it skyward. He pretended to shoot it in midair, imitating a soldier's aim with his fingers. He pictured himself as a fighter in a distant war, hidden in broad daylight, in the middle of battle, although he looked more like a lost boy the dogs regarded with pity.

He went into the house with dirt all over his clothes, in his hair. He flopped onto the couch and looked at his hands:

a smear of shit. Enraged, he went to his room and scraped his right palm against a page in his Spanish notebook. He saw that it had been half a year since he'd written a word. He returned to the kitchen and realized only then that there was no water. He stood there, sweating, with the smell and the smudge and the page stuck to his hand like a shadow.

The kids' house was the final stop for the water tanker that serviced the town once a week. It wouldn't come by till after four. That morning, Catalina had left for school with a canteen filled with the very last of their potable water. Patricio, meanwhile, settled for taking the final swig of soda from the bottle and shitting in a bag. He closed his eyes. He breathed, remembering the time he overheard his Aunt Carmela talking about him on the phone to a friend. He's lost, poor thing, he heard her say from the bathroom. Hopeless. I'm thinking of taking Catalina to live with me. The house looked like it hadn't been cleaned in years, blackened walls, broken windows, kitchen caked in dust, loose earth seated there at the table.

Patricio went into the yard, spit into his hands, and dragged them over the ground. He'd put on a pair of red underpants and swapped his sweaty T-shirt for a button-down. He'd started wearing his father's clothes a while ago. Sometimes Catalina imitated him and said she was the dad too. She'd give him instructions. Simulate a thick mustache and deliver sermons on life. He'd smile when his sister played at being an actress. He pictured her on TV. He'd dress her up in his head as a gypsy girl, an Italian girl, a girl from Chiloé, and pair her with some other equally theatrical kid, and have them push and chase each other around some desert, forest, or circus tent.

Patricio liked those fables as much as she did. He'd developed a taste for them. Ever since she was little, Pedro and María had asked Catalina to tell stories, show them her drawings, explain what the characters were up to. She'd improvise for a while, and then her parents would comment on the result, as if they were a team of editors or screenwriters. Several noteworthy figures emerged and rooted themselves into the family imagination: the Bald Hen, the Disordered Brothers, Sir Pepe Spots, Mr. Guachicamote, Brown Sugar Dog. María loved it, played along with her daughter. She was the casting director. If the story was good, she'd say, it would end up on TV. Patricio always occupied a distant if attentive role in these games. He ignored his mother when she invited him to join in. He'd retreat to the yard and imagine wars waged with sticks and stones. Assemble plastic soldiers and smash them with rocks. He'd narrate the battle aloud like a Spanish news broadcaster, mimicking their whistled Iberian s sounds: "Cannonballs assail the island from the docks. Barefoot soldiers flee for their lives." His mother loved to see him playing by himself and would leave him alone. Now, instead of playing games, Patricio entertained himself by thinking aloud, for the company—like someone who talks to animals—or for the simple pleasure of hearing what the words sounded like.

He walked for a long time. He would walk for walking's sake: almost a year of days advancing in a circle, with little else to do than climb the hill. But if some forest ranger asked what he was up to on this side of the fence, he'd say that he was looking for his lost dog Celerino, although Pedro had actually killed the dog one morning when the mutt came home with rabies. After several hours of trudging uphill through the brush, throat parched and scratchy, Patricio sat in the shade of a eucalyptus. In that position, the sun still found a way to touch the tip of his sneaker. He pulled his knees in. Stared into the distance. The tree plantation seemed to sketch the horizon line. He leaned his head against the trunk. The world is a lost cause, he thought, as he listened to the wind, and the murmur of the leaves coaxed his eyes shut.

Suddenly, the roar of engines woke him. Night was falling and Patricio hurtled down the slope, heeding a strange intuition. He wondered if Catalina was already home, if she'd bolted the front door. When he finally made it back, he picked up two old tires, stacked one on top of the other, hoisted himself up to the roof, and shielded his eyes to squint. He saw two black SUVs approaching, like the kind in detective shows. Frightened, he came down in a single leap. His clothes were reduced to dirty shreds from the impact with the tires. He rushed inside, latched the door, hid under the table.

"Cata? Catalina, are you home?"

They parked outside. Patricio heard the doors opening

and several men—he couldn't tell how many—got out and made their way toward the house.

Three brisk knocks on the door.

"Hello? Hel-lo?"

From under the table, Patricio couldn't tell who was calling, but he saw figures peering in through the windows, swift shadows, like dogs in the dark.

"We're going to leave this here!" one of the intruders declared, as if he could tell that someone was listening on the other side.

Then the men returned to the vehicles, the engines revved, and the lights retreated along the road.

Patricio waited some ten minutes before resolving to open the door. He found five boxes on the ground. One contained a Smart TV, the other a PlayStation 5, both brand new, and the others were filled with groceries. There was also a book resting on top of the boxes.

"*The Compendium of Pedro the Vast*," he read aloud, touching the title on the cover.

He looked up, couldn't see anything on the road. Half a kilometer down, he saw the lights in the neighbor's house switch on. Night had come, and a few drops of weak rain began to fall. He nudged the boxes inside with his foot and flung the book into the yard. It fell to the ground by the empty chicken coop.

As he closed the door, the light bulb in the dining room, dark for weeks, turned on again.

⚙

THE RAIN TRACED subtle diagonal lines across the windows. Sweeping plains expanded along the highway, interrupted only by occasional houses, animals, and barns scattered erratically over the grassland. Amid so much space, the sky enjoyed a different kind of openness, and the clouds strained to gather. The van progressed toward Punta Arenas, nervously driven by Señora Marta, who gripped the wheel with both hands and occasionally kissed the small medallion of Our Lady of Mount Carmel she wore around her right wrist.

Giovanna, meanwhile, served as interpreter for the questions and answers among the group of foreigners, and as their impromptu tour guide, responding with her eyes fixed on the road. Every so often, pointing to something beyond the highway, Giovanna would ask something too: the purpose for some fenced-in fortress, the common name of certain birds, the lifespan of those native trees. I don't know, mijita, I don't know, Señora Marta would respond, looking straight ahead, sweating a little, and then Giovanna would make something up to sate the visitors' curiosity, hovering as best they could by the windows of the van to admire the starkness of the landscape.

The clicks of the digital cameras matched the dripping on the aluminum roof as the old Nissan Caravan entered the city. After a series of sudden halts at red lights, the engine cutting out at green lights, honks, shouted insults, and holymotherofgods, the group of scientists reached the cemetery.

The rain had stopped.

"How are you feeling?" Giovanna asked the group of

foreigners as they stretched out on the sidewalk. Andrea smiled behind them, her blond hair disheveled by the austral breeze. Everyone seemed excited to start the trip.

Before they made their way into the cemetery, Giovana asked them to meet back at the van within an hour. Señora Marta stayed inside the vehicle, leaning back in her seat, eyes closed, relieved to have gotten this far without an accident.

Giovanna and Andrea zipped their windbreakers and walked slowly along the monumental cypress-lined boulevards of the mortuary labyrinth, letting the group scatter freely. They poked around the graves, surprised at the different sizes and providence of surnames and mausoleums. At one point, Andrea moved to take her hand, but Giovanna shifted—a swift, subtle gesture—and pointed to the name carved on a tombstone: "Teléfona Palacio." They laughed softly, not wanting to offend the deceased, as Giovanna took a photo of Andrea making a "Call me" gesture with her hand. They passed the enormous crypt of Sara Braun, the graveyard's namesake, which was teeming with tourists dazzled by its peculiar gold dome, as if stolen from a mosque. And then they found themselves in a place that felt more like a botanic garden than a cemetery: vines scaled the broken glass from the outside, and inside you could see all kinds of cacti and hanging plants. Giovanna jotted some things down in her notebook as Andrea took photos.

"Look at me," she said suddenly, and her brown eyes were startled by the click of the analog camera.

Then they came to an aisle where the cypress boughs were naked, dry, dark, like survivors of a fire. Andrea asked if a fungus was the culprit. Giovanna touched the branches, then sniffed and licked her fingers before she said no.

"Might be aphids," she added, scanning the blotches on the cypress. "Or maybe the trees just caught the urge to die."

·☼·

WHEN SHE OPENED the door, Catalina found her brother parked in front of a huge TV screen in the middle of the living room, intent on a virtual soccer game. Without a blink, she set her backpack onto the table, sat down beside him, and asked, "How do you play?"

From then on, Patricio found the patience to teach his sister how to control the players, one at a time; to kick the ball back and forth between them rather than simply shooting for the goal whenever she had the ball in her power. Pato said she could skip school that week, and they practiced for two full days until Catalina finally managed a tie with a last-minute goal. All their prior matches had ended in defeat, most by a landslide. Her joy was uncontainable. Yeeesss! Yeeeess! Take that, Pato! One to one! And she ran around the house, arms outstretched at her sides like a plane.

"Easy, small fry. You can celebrate when you beat me."

Patricio hit *start* and they began a new game.

She never asked him where all the stuff had come from.

She sprawled on the massage chair and cranked it up as high as it could go, darted around the house while menacing Patricio with the immersion blender, crawled into the dryer, took long hot showers, then spent hours popping birds, fruits, and multicolored balls on her phone, and sometimes, when she had the house to herself, she'd grind up bugs and dirt in the food processor. The boxes brought new things every week. Catalina would wait for her brother to open them, inspecting each new device with fascination, then ask him to teach her how to use it.

"Look, this one has two buttons. Which kind of coffee do you want, big or small?"

"Big!" she'd exclaim.

Then he'd press the green button and the machine would serve up a tall latte, which Catalina would carry off happily to her room. In this way, the house slowly filled with electrical appliances, groceries, clothes, bicycles, toys, and a white envelope with a sickle-shaped seal, packed with orange bills, first thing every Monday morning. The books that accompanied the gifts were piled up and forgotten in the chicken coop. The birds hopped about on top of them, shitting and pecking insistently.

Patricio never tried to investigate. Better not, he told himself: What if the boxes stopped coming? Let the fanatics do whatever they want with their father. In any case, the pantry was stocked, Catalina took the bus to school, and he had money to spend at whim. He stored the bills and cards in a shoebox in his bedroom, and every so often he'd tell Catalina that their dad was being taken care of in another country. That he'd been abducted by Martians. Or eaten by the chupacabras. And did she want some more bread with avocado. And don't take that tone with him. And he was the man of the house now.

Catalina stared into her hot chocolate.

"How about a soccer game?" he asked, setting his mug on the table.

"Okay."

☼

WHEN THE GROUP finally reached Chilota Bay, the dock at Porvenir, the foreigners had recovered their spirit of adventure. Their wan-faced queasiness aboard the ferry gave way to strawberry-red cheeks, and they were eager to hear all about the little houses with corrugated tin roofs and vivid harbor hues they could glimpse on the horizon, scattered like notes of tempera across the monotonous steppe. At over eighty-five degrees Fahrenheit, the heat quickly induced forgetfulness. Giovanna kept putting on and taking off her jacket as the van crossed the southernmost region of the world.

Señora Marta, meanwhile, had left her nerves behind, possibly because she faced no obstacles ahead: along CH-257 and Y-85, two snaking stretches of 136 and 159 kilometers, respectively, straining toward the south of Tierra del Fuego, there were more sheep, camelids, cyclists, horses, and roadrunners than cars. So she had no trouble now responding to the guests' many inquiries, and even engaged them in conversation, chitchatting away in well-mannered English.

But after the strenuous crossing of the strait, the troops were weary. Only Giovanna's eyes were still fixed on the road. She spoke intermittently with Señora Marta about the strangeness of the weather, the nationality of the visitors, the nature of her work—for seven hours straight.

At last, when the van's wheels slowed in front of the Vicuña Hostel, the group awoke to a glorious spectacle. At that hour, the sun's final threads sliced across the tip of the lenga beech grove that marked the beginning of the park, and their orange canopies took on the density of rouge.

It was magnificent, but there was barely time for photos. Beneath the trees approached the figure of Don Santiago, the forest ranger, who made his way toward the team a few steps behind Oliver, his enormous and bedraggled sheepdog. They'd have to set up camp before dark.

Aided by Don Santiago, Giovanna, Andrea, and Davon, the youngest Brit, they took up the task of pitching the five individual tents, plus the one huge tent where they'd install their research equipment. But as the wind blew in with deafening force, they eventually needed the help of the entire group, Señora Marta included, to secure them.

The job was done around nine. It wasn't raining, but a cold wind crept under their clothes. Don Santiago invited them to share some yerba maté in his house, which was heated by a woodstove. The research team trailed single-file behind the ranger, rubbing their hands as they stepped inside and waited their turn for the bathroom.

The silence was engrossing. The guests were enthralled by the rhythm of the fire as it crackled behind the old wrought-iron of the stove, which was periodically fed by small logs that Don Santiago had cut with near-geometric precision. The water boiled. Their host removed the kettle from the hot surface, set out ember tortillas to heat on the same spot, and delicately replenished the maté with water. Giovanna received it when he passed it to her, took a noisy sip, and returned it immediately with a curt "Thanks." Don Santiago shot her an offended glance and raised his eyebrows. Andrea intervened at once, rushing to explain that her friend hadn't meant to be rude; it was just that she was from way up north: They only drink coffee there, she said, before switching to English for the group and explaining the rites of the fire, step by step.

Santiago softened at the sight of the foreigners and their awkward, theatrical solemnity as they passed the maté around in a circle, as if they'd been invited to participate in some endemic ancestral ceremony. Sitting across from her, Giovanna looked at Andrea with gratitude. They drank in silence as Santiago stoked the fire and the kick of the herb restored heat and spark to their bodies.

After a couple full rotations, Andrea gestured to Giovanna. The group rose behind her, thanked Santiago, and retreated into the stark cold of the steppe.

Half an hour later, once all the others were arranged in their respective sleeping bags, Giovanna stroked Andrea's hand, pressed like soft fabric to her cheek. Andrea stared up at the roof of the tent, which rippled with a rivery sound.

"I really mean it," Giovanna said. "It's so nice you're here."

A few minutes later, lights out, her faint voice still reaching:

"Are you awake?"

"Mmm."

"Nothing, it's nothing."

"What is it."

"It's just that I remembered how when I was little, there was this game I liked to play before I fell asleep. I've never told anyone about it. I tried to focus on something I was thinking about and then work backward, thought by thought, as if I were following a thread into the idea I was thinking about before. And then the one before it. And so on until I made my way all the way back to something where there was nothing. The thread snapped. And then I'd lie there with a piece of string floating around in my mind."

Andrea rolled over to face her, still half asleep, inching closer in her sleeping bag. She gave Giovanna a kiss between the mouth and cheek, rested her head on her shoulder.

"That's beautiful...Let's get some sleep?"

"Sure, yeah," Giovanna said, eyes still fixed on the roof of the tent as it rippled hard, listening to the wind sweep over the plains and plains all around them. She closed her eyes with its impetus. She felt safe, in a way. Safe in her belonging to the landscape that surrounded her. That let her listen to herself, slowly, as if thinking were nothing but a simple, measurable murmur, loose pieces fitting together, every so often, into a ring, and then sundering, dissolving in the light.

⚙

ONE AFTERNOON, PATRICIO WOKE to a sequence of knocks on the front door. He went into his sister's room and found it empty. Confused, he zipped his down jacket and planted himself squarely in the center of the living room. Through the window, he could see a group of men stationed outside two black SUVs. More knocks in heavy, rhythmic triplets. He took a deep breath and turned the knob.

On the other side stood a lean man, slightly taller than he was.

"Good evening, brother," he said, his lips tugging into a face that Patricio took for robotic cordiality. "My name is Balthasar. I've been eager to meet you."

"I don't have any brothers," Patricio replied as if cracking a branch with his voice.

"We're all brothers in the vast." Patricio noted a eucalyptus capsule hanging against his purple tunic. "Do you know who I am?"

"The ugly motherfucker who kidnapped my dad."

Behind Balthasar, four men stood beside the black vehicles. They didn't seem to be hiding any presents. All of them fixed Patricio with the compassionate, intimidating gaze of religious fanatics.

Balthasar smiled faintly and went on: "Oh, no, that's not the case at all."

"What the fuck do you want?"

"I need you to come with us."

Patricio took a few steps back. Suddenly, it was as if he were running, craning his neck to track a pass kicked to him from the other end of the field, as if his sister were feinting with Messi at the entrance to the virtual arena and his own hand were sweating on the controller, as if his father were teaching him to hunt rabbits and he had to hold his breath before those wide black eyes that stared at him hard before he put them out, as if someone were pushing up into the space between his anus and his testicles, as if his mother were slapping him, as if a cold sweat were trickling down his back, as if a tremble in his chin, as if a hint of tears, as if they were suddenly about to kidnap him, too, in his own house, as if it were the easiest thing in the world.

He heard a cat mewling on the roof. Patricio gathered saliva in his mouth.

"Okay, let's go," he said, closing the door behind him.

· ☼ ·

THE DOOR WAS ENCLOSED by a broad wooden fence strung with electrical wiring. Two men in purple tunics opened the gate. Inside, devotees moved about, absorbed in their tasks, murmuring things he couldn't hear. The place felt modest, and at the same time its decorations suggested some kind of lineage; the style of the buildings evoked German colonies, surrounded by rows and rows of eucalyptus saplings. They had Patricio get out of the SUV and walk through a door with a sign that read THE VAST. They closed it delicately behind them and left him in the dark. He could barely make out the room. He groped at the edges, the tips of what seemed like wooden statues. Then, little by little, a fluorescent glow lit up the space.

The hall was compact, though the ceilings were high. The scent of the eucalyptus branches hung on the walls made him think of his father boiling leaves in the kitchen. And when he looked ahead, he saw him, seated in a wicker chair, although his body seemed to have been tossed there like a sack. Still unable to entirely believe what he was seeing, before he could rub his eyes or pinch himself, Patricio heard his father say: "Come here, son." But the voice wasn't like Pedro's voice. Not as he remembered it. Advancing toward him, Pato was hit with an acrid smell, like rotten fruit. Once he was closer, he noted that his father's face showed clear signs of emaciation. It reminded him of a wax figure. A quick, cold thread shot down his shoulders. He felt a pang of disgust. It was as if Pedro's skin, damp, were melting.

Patricio shook as he stood there, tears choking his breath. Pedro said nothing. A silence spread between them. Then he pricked his ears and saw that his father's right hand was starting to move. Beside the chair was a small table laid with religious paraphernalia, plus one of the Sudoku puzzles Pato used to give him. Uneasy, Patricio followed Pedro's hand with his eyes as it picked up a pencil and began to press the tip into the notepad. He moved closer, opened it to the first page, and let the hand fill the table like an automaton. Instead of numbers, the hand wrote letters in the squares. Slow rows forming words. The writing absorbed Patricio's full attention until the message was ready. Then he felt a terror like the kind he felt in a certain memory of his mother: the two of them sitting together by the woodstove as she rocked him, still small, in her arms, and told him the story of the little boy with spurs.[14]

---

14   In the *Folkloric Dictionary of the Bíobío Region*, compiled by Alfonso Alcalde, it reads: "Once upon a time, on a night in the country-side, there was a small, abandoned boy. He'd fallen off the wagon and his father hadn't noticed. They were on their way back from a tavern. The little boy had felt happy because he liked seeing his father dance and drink into the night, but now he was lost and all alone on the way home, and he was sad. His face was covered in mud and the backs of his hands were scratched. He didn't know what to do. Suddenly, he saw something gleaming a few steps down the road. He walked over to it, his eyes shining, and recognized a pair of metal spurs. He picked them up and thought of his father. He remembered that his father couldn't sleep without hanging his spurs over the bed. So his father, no matter how drunk he was, would have no choice but to retrace his steps until he found them. That made the boy stop crying. He tied the spurs to his little shoes and began to dance and clap in the middle of the road. His steps kicked up dust and the boy's clothes and body were soon covered in dirt, so much dirt that his skin split open and his entire body turned into a single cloud of dust, scattered by the air and the wind. In his transformation, the spurs fell to the ground and the boy couldn't dance anymore. This made him infinitely sad. When his father finally found the spurs, he heard his son crying and realized what he had done. In his

The page said the following:

O	M	Y	S	O	N	F	L	E
E	F	R	O	M	T	H	E	V
A	S	T	L	I	G	H	T	O
F	M	Y	V	O	I	C	E	B
L	A	Z	E	B	U	R	N	I
N	G	M	E	S	O	A	R	I
N	G	O	V	E	R	T	H	E
F	I	R	E	T	H	A	T	C
O	M	E	S	F	O	R	M	E

The door opened. Two collegians seized him by the shoulders and hauled him out. Sobbing, Patricio managed to tear out the page, stuffed it into his pocket, and left through the door of the hall, his body as if underwater.

It was the last time he ever saw his father.

The sky was coated in a single gray smudge. Balthasar ushered him into an SUV that set out for home. Up above, in the distance, Patricio glimpsed a strange black ring that floated among the clouds. Lower down, the repetition of the eucalyptuses formed a hypnotic sequence, and he soon fell

---

wretchedness, he cleaved the spurs into his neck and the blood streamed down until it formed a pool from which two blue roses bloomed. Ever since, if you're traveling on a dirt road at night and hear the weeping of a little boy, you'd better say seven Lord's Prayers, look up at the sky, and clap a cueca rhythm with the palms of your hands, so that the little boy with spurs can keep dancing."

asleep, leaning against the back window. He woke face-down in his own bed, still dressed, a bit sweaty. He leapt up and tore around the house, calling his sister.

But he was alone. He still felt his father's strange, befuddled voice, dragged out and scattered by the wind. Following that voice, he went out.

⚙

CATALINA WAS PERCHED in the massage chair, eating some bread with pâté and trying to beat Real Madrid with Barcelona.

"Where have you been?" Patricio asked, pulling the front door shut.

"At Aunt Carmela's." When she lied, his sister's squinted eyes reminded him of his mother's.

Nervous, Patricio went into his room for a warmer layer and grabbed a lighter. Before he left again, Catalina asked for some hot chocolate.

"Where are you going?" she asked afterward, her mug resting on a glass side table, eyes still intent on the screen, as Patricio zipped up his sweatshirt and tugged on the hood.

"To buy something. I'll be right back."

"To buy a car?"

Patricio felt a shiver. He thought of the gas canisters he'd parked outside the house and squeezed the lighter hard in his pocket.

His sister paused the game and looked at him.

He smiled and pocketed his keys.

"I'm going to buy an airplane," he said, lifting his thumb and index finger to his lips as if taking a hit.

It's the indefinite continuation of existence. Every body needs other bodies, to die and to regenerate. Its vastness entails joining their heads, following the restless murmur conveyed by wind to home, that secret body, root of water, that extirpates the tongue from its cage and flees in ash as the forests decamp to another universe.

THE WALK HAD STARTED early in muted rainfall and seventy percent humidity. Led by Giovanna, the team hiked two hours south of camp until they reached lot ten: an area abundant in ñirre shrubs, lenga beeches, coigüe beeches, and topsoil moistened by beaver dams.

That was where they found the first specimens.

"Look at me, tell me what you found," Andrea instructed, half her head concealed by the camera.

"This *Cyttaria* I'm holding is also known as 'Indian bread.' Long ago, the inhabitants of these woods would gather and eat them in the spring and summer." Giovanna held up a mushroom that looked like a medlar fruit. She offered it to her colleague, who stood outside the frame beside Andrea. "Try it, Richard." The Brit bit into the mushroom and looked surprised by the cottony texture. "It's sweet, right?" she continued, eyes wide and enthralled as a child's, and he nodded with pleasure.

On this expedition, each member of the team was after something different. Davon, for example, scraped the ground with a rake in search of truffles. He had the most difficult task: Such mushrooms grow underground and tend to be identified by the noses of specially trained dogs and pigs. Davon was relying on his intuition alone. Even so, Andrea managed to record the moment when the young redheaded man scraped at the root of a lenga beech and unveiled a *Thaxterogaster*: two white spheres gleaming like diamonds in the damp soil.

Marjorie, meanwhile, was studying the genus *Cortinarius,* whose species sprouted in broad daylight all over the park. Many hadn't yet been classified, so her happy chore was to name and date them, an official christening for the sake of science. Andrea followed her as she filled a small burlap sack with a diverse array of mushrooms, offering up little exclamations of delight in her fussy English.

Then there was Richard, a mycologist with nearly forty years of experience under his belt, who was responsible for analyzing the connection between the mushrooms and the park's endemic flora. Cloaked in an olive-green raincoat, the old man strode through the woods with a precision magnifier and a Swiss Army knife, hands clasped behind him. He cut samples of roots, bark, fruiting bodies of many forms: convex, sunken, navel-shaped, breast-shaped, shapes that sometimes resembled tiny beehives or pieces of coral.

As he explained to the camera, eyes shining under a crimson hat, every life hidden under those forms had its own distinct function. "It's one thing to describe an organism according to what it looks like and quite another to understand its relationship with other beings in its environment. All of these mushrooms are bound to the trees by their roots. They provide water and nutrients, receiving vitamins and carbon dioxide in return. Trees can communicate through mushrooms, like a kind of internet." He pointed to the bottom end of a *Cortinarius flammuloides* species, endemic to the region. "What we typically see of mushrooms is just their sex—reddish, multiform swellings that release spores to reproduce. The whole mushroom functions like a vast network, spanning kilometers: Its slender threads silently connect the forest while transforming its waste into new earth."

The rain intensified. Giovanna found Andrea and instructed the team to take the trail south. Little by little, the sound of water pummeling the leaves gave way to a waft of sea breeze.

Giovanna collected lichen. She was researching whether the symbiosis between mushrooms and algae affects the way in which lichen communicates with other organisms. In the electrical charges that travel through mycelium, she saw signs of a process much like neuronal activation. Something moved about in this transit: information, locations, desires. A language of subterranean impulses. Giovanna wondered what happened when the mushroom joined together with something else. Talking in bed the night before, Andrea had asked what kind of words such a language might have.

She asked, snuggled against Giovanna in the same sleeping bag, "If a mushroom were to colonize a human brain, would it think the same things as we do?"

Giovanna hadn't answered, just shifted on top of her and started kissing her neck. But later, as Andrea snored, the question nagged at her, so much so that she had a dream in which she was analyzing a white moss mote whose cells, under the zoom of the microscope, turned out to be millions of eyes.

Half an hour later, the group reunited with the Strait of Magellan, this time on the opposite end of the Isla Grande de Tierra del Fuego.

The panorama was remarkable. Giovanna stared out at the islands, ancient heaps of elephant skin peeking through dense vegetation, and imagined an age when an interlacing of mushrooms and rocks covered the earth. She stood there for a few minutes, admiring it all, picturing eight-meter towers of pleated granite that rose up like independent statues, as the subtle threads of a *Tortotubus protuberans* embraced the mineral from the inside, prompting fresh water to burgeon there and narrow its walls, travel lower down, burrow into the rock from behind, flatten the ground for animals and plants to then parcel out the world among themselves, each securing its own essential place. When algae and amphibia fell captive to sexual desire, she thought, mushrooms must have held their perspective steady, already kissing mammals and plants as they slumbered in the open earth, already washing their wounded chests with enzymes, dividing them, making them more magnificent. This allowed fungi to expand in the shape of a grand idea, as if the earth above were something like the wall of the skull; below, a bottomless lake. This was how they grew, in scores of directions, groping blindly along, seizing at roots and buried bodies.

Giovanna stood transfixed by the view until the wind struck her in the face. Then she trailed behind the group, which struggled with the uphill climb toward the Timaukel forest, as the water and rocks conspired to trip them. Her eyes periodically drifted back to the landscape and then sought Andrea, who was entertained by the sounds of the Brits up ahead, a string of *oops, oops* they blurted when their hiking boots slipped and they found themselves sunk to their ankles once again.

By early evening, the thrilled and exhausted foragers made it back to camp with an ample stash of samples to classify. Giovanna stopped at the tent to drop off her bag. As she walked to Don Santiago's for a shower, she noticed a thin black ring high in the sky, sketched like a burn among the clouds.

She caught a pleasant smell as she returned to the tent. A few meters beyond the site, Richard was cooking dinner in an enormous pot on the fire: soup with morels, onion, garlic, pepper, potato, zucchini, other edible mushrooms. Davon donated one of his truffles, which made the broth into something wondrous. All seven of them ate outside, chatting around the fire about the marvels of the place. Above them, a spilled cumulus of stars offered another spectacle. Giovanna rested her head on Andrea's shoulder, captivated by the heat of the fire and the meal. Her wet hair slowly dried.

The next morning, the group threw themselves into the onerous task of classifying the specimens. They worked in a tent they'd equipped for this purpose, thanks to an electric generator rented from Don Santiago. Inside it, each researcher had access to a varied arsenal of scientific instruments.

After breakfast, as the scientists set out to analyze their mushrooms in earnest, Giovanna stayed behind to help their host. She washed dishes in water so cold it hurt her fingers and told Don Santiago about their expedition the day before.

"So you were walking around lot ten, I see?"

"Yes! We managed to cover almost a quarter of it," she told him proudly. "Isn't it beautiful?"

She felt her phone vibrate in the back pocket of her jeans. She shut off the water and wiped her hands on a dish towel to answer.

Oliver, who'd been sleeping by the woodstove, began to bark at Giovanna with great insistence. Don Santiago had to drag him out by the collar and shut the door. Sorry, miss, this old dog's on his last legs, he ventured, worried by the color that had drained from Giovanna's face. She covered her free ear to hear better.

"An explosion? I'm not following, Mom—what did you say? What white fire?"

Uneasy from the call, she returned to the lab tent, began to organize her workspace, and recognized a kind of archaeology in the task her colleagues were undertaking: as if everything to which she'd devoted the past fifteen years of her life was now reduced to documenting the origins of a past. She glanced at Marjorie, who waved cheerily as she wrapped two mushrooms in aluminum foil. All of a sudden, she felt the ground shifting underfoot. Dizzy, she decided to step out. Andrea, who was reading in the shade of a ñirre tree a few meters beyond the tents, noticed something off about her. She asked what was wrong, but Giovanna just fluttered a dismissive hand and went back into the tent.

Her phone rang again. A friend told her about an enormous fire rising from the south of Bíobío toward Concepción. She said the authorities were advising the evacuation of the city. Giovanna hung up, set her phone aside, and fell back onto her sleeping bag, rested her head on a backpack full of clothes. The news hit her as if a bubble, a membrane enclosing her beyond the scope of historical time, had burst and left her in free fall. She lay there, eyes on the ceiling, watching the blue of the plastic change with the light. Something in the air was blowing against her. Her limbs felt heavy, her chest tight. She was probably thinking about hundreds of foxes and owls fleeing the woods, or imagining half of

Concepción up in flames. She stayed still. Wordless. Steady. Dry-eyed. Her breath slowed to a minimum, as if her body were no longer her business. As if her will were guided by a single ironic wind.[15]

☼

THE SERMON WAS about to start. Pedro, despite his state of health, was encouraged by his devotees to take the pulpit. The closest circle of collegians got him ready. They lifted him from his chair, rubbed his wounds with eucalyptus balm, wafted the smoke from the leaves onto his tunic, split fruit and raised it to his nose. Pedro didn't react. He seemed to be far away from his body, dragged along by a sort of automatism. Balthasar, extremely nervous about this behavior, had believed that seeing his son would help Pedro recover his energy for the evening sermon. It troubled him to see the prophet's further decline. He settled Pedro into

---

15 On the other end of the territory, no few words were uttered about a wild firestorm, "with ultra-rapid propagations of up to 8,200 hectares per hour and exceptional heat intensities of over 60,000 kW/h, in addition to local winds of up to 130 km/hour, similar to those observed in catastrophes documented in Chile, the United States, Greece, and Australia at the end of the last decade." Firefighters and emergency brigades were sent in. An enormous tanker plane was brought in. But no specialist was able to interpret the white clouds, those gargantuan cumuli of spores billowing up from underground, covering and penetrating the ash and the bodies calcified by flames, where each served as substrate for reproduction.

his wheelchair and pushed him from his home to the main temple, straightening his faith with the vigor of the wind that swept at his thin hair, glancing up again at the ring of black smoke that had hovered in the firmament for several hours now.

Inside, the hall was packed with collegians, waiting, singing, as others circulated, swinging eucalyptus censers in the air. Balthasar appeared onstage, received their applause, and asked the congregation to sit.

"My brothers and sisters, I breathe you here."

The collegians rose to their feet again. In his speech, Balthasar undertook to assuage certain rumors about Pedro's health.

"Now is not the time to heed the separate. Our Vastness would not wish us to be ill, would do us no wrong, would not bring us into contact with anyone unwell. What kind of God does not tend to His children? What kind of shepherd leaves his flock to their fate? Pedro will disprove all these jealous words. Soon, he will make his own voice heard to you."

The hall filled with applause and enthusiastic shouting. The evening sun slanted in through a skylight, sketching small eaves of shadow around the pulpit. Pedro entered from one side of the stage. The collegians had been awaiting his sermons all week, working hard to keep the Door up and running: tending the gardens; making artisanal eucalyptus products like notebooks, oils, and creams to sell in downtown

Curanilahue; gathering fruit; keeping watch at the edges of the property by night. A sermon was the site of the miracle. In this temple, they'd seen children cured of aphasia, stutterers declaiming fluidly out of the blue, mutilated bodies whose hacked-off tongues suddenly resprouted in their mouths like cactus blossoms. Those were the rumors heard in the city. The sound of Pedro's voice sent some devotees into a trance. They'd jump around in a state of bliss and imitate the master's dictations, arms held high over their heads.

Pedro took a step forward and it was as if the wind had slammed the windows shut. He walked to the center of the stage. Makeup and all, there was no denying that he looked much worse. The audience grew uneasy as his silence lengthened. The prophet stared ahead, trying to speak, but he was overcome with a violent coughing fit.

The collegians stirred, anxious, and as some rose to assist Pedro, Balthasar's fear knotted tight around his tongue. He tried to calm the crowd, but the words caught in his throat, refused to come out.

And then Pedro's voice resounded like the cracking of a glacier. Nothing to do but press their hands to their ears and watch the horrific spectacle: a white filament pierced his skin like the fine threads of a skein of moss, fissuring him with wounds that released a rush of stems through his eyes, arms, and cheeks, and a long, dark sporocarp emerged from behind his head, rising up and exuding the scent of forest detritus, as

Pedro's throat swelled and burst into a cloud of spores that covered the entire hall in a single white mantle.[16]

·❀·

A TALL WOODEN BARRIER, electric fencing. A couple of dry sparrows strung from the wire. Their toasted plumage and white eyes warned: Cross with caution. Patricio took a small, see-through packet out of his pocket. He put the contents in a pipe and burned it. Shaken, he prodded the planks until he found a loose one. Then he maneuvered his body to the other side and dragged the canisters behind him.

The darkness let him move easily around the place. He was surprised by the silence: He could hear his own pulse in

---

16 Unsuspecting of infection, some families of Chilean and Mapuche peasant farmers stayed on this side of the territory, glimpsing, from the Nahuelbuta mountain range, the cities consumed by fire, their view blanketed by a dense white fog. Over time, these communities adapted to a starker lifestyle, a collective, foraging-based economy. So said José Liendo, the no less vast, after Pedro, in his second testimony: "What hails from here is unknown to the separate, has seen nothing like it in a long time. We rise and find our food hanging from the trees, calling our name. We bathe in the river as soon as it proffers its current to us, and there we find the vigor to work in tranquility all day long. If we grow tired or take ill, we find medicine in the brush, which grows unirrigated of its own accord. Here there is no one who leads or thinks for the others. We are all part of a single sameness. When someone dies, it is because the water in his body must be cleaned. We dig a hole, leave him in the ground, and a pilunhueque, huayo, or litre plant may grow there to protect him. The roots of the plants convey his blood to the river, and then it rains. To be on this side of the forest, friend, is to be more than one head. Do you believe me when I say that I can see you now with the eyes of every single bird on the branches up above us?"

his ears. He didn't see a single light on, not a single person out and about, but figured they must be gathered in some ceremony or other. All the better. He liked the thought of catching them by surprise.

With the composure he'd always shown as a boy, when he played in the woods till late and made his way home by himself, Patricio entered the main temple and crossed the shadowed room. He held up a lighter and read AUDITORIUM written above a door. When he stepped in, the density of the air was what struck him first. A strange smell, like rotten vegetables in the fridge. He covered his nose. As his eyes adjusted to the dark, he noticed a peculiar white crust covering the floor and walls like lichen or dried cum. His right sneaker bumped against something that seemed to be a body lying face-down. Alarmed, he took a few steps back, feeling his way along the wall until he found the switch, and then the hall brightened to the erratic rhythm of the fluorescent tubes.

Patricio threw up at the sight before him. He fell to his knees, hands flat beside a white-eyed man, skin petrified by a fine coat of mold. Sobbing, retching, he pissed himself a bit. Bile trickled down his chest and he had to wipe his mouth with the sleeve of his sweatshirt. Struggling to stand, he staggered back against the wall, and only then could he see in perspective. A pavilion of corpses caked in white dust. Patricio recognized his father in the middle of the stage, his neck split open, his body latticed with sinister branches flowering right before his eyes.

He struggled desperately to uncap the canisters and drag

them out of the temple. In his panic, he spattered some on his pants.

Outside, he lit the trickle of gasoline. As he tucked the lighter back into his pocket, he stumbled backward into a small body.

He turned his head and saw her.

"What the fuck are you doing here?"

Catalina shrank away, frightened by her brother's reaction and wild, bloodshot eyes. "Are you following me? Tell me you didn't go in, tell me you weren't in there. Fucking answer me!" he shouted, shaking her by the shoulders.

Cata started to cry. She didn't get what was going on, she said, why hadn't he come home, how long had he been hiding their dad's letters, did he think she was stupid, those presents didn't fall from the sky, she knew, she'd looked it up online, if Dad lived here then why hadn't they come to see him, why did Patricio have throw-up on his face, had he peed his pants or something.

"We have to get out of here!" Patricio grabbed her arm and pulled her away from the temple.

Then he saw the gas stains on his sweatpants and yanked them off, moments before the church transformed into a single enormous flame.

The roar flung them headfirst onto the ground.

Dazed by the explosion, Patricio sat up and gathered his sister in his arms. The blaze sent up a mass of smoke that muddled the exit: The buildings of the Door seemed to triple around them, the smoke erased cardinal directions. The siblings darted in circles. A few trees strained their limbs to help them. Catalina pointed and urged her brother to look up at the eucalyptuses. The branches, the branches! she yelled, as Patricio, bewildered, jerked his head from side to side. Over there, Pato, look! she sobbed into his shoulder, squeezing her eyes shut, hitting him on the chest, until her brother finally saw the electric fence.

He broke into a run before he could help her to her feet, just dragged her by the arm. More explosions sounded from where they fled. Branches ablaze, crashing down onto majestic ripples of ember. Patricio tripped on a rock as he turned to watch them.

Pato! Catalina screamed as he fell forward into the electric fence, his hands catching in the fence, seized with terrible spasms. She ran over and threw her arms around him, heaved him toward her until he was free.

Patricio opened his eyes. The world was slow to reach him, his senses as jumbled as if he'd just lifted his head out of the water.[17] He struggled to sit and found his sister lying on the ground. Her eyes were closed, her cheek gashed.

---

17 One morning when he was small, Patricio had an experience that the whole family took to calling "the well incident." It was early and Pedro had sent him to get water for Catalina's bath. He stepped out into the yard, cloaked in fog, and walked out to the well on the other side of

the lot. Along the way, he felt like someone was whispering sad, strange things in his ear. He tried to ignore them, remembering something I once explained to him when I was still myself: "We all have a river inside us, sweet boy. It's nice to look at. To sit at the edge and hear the fish bumping into the rocks, catch one in your hand, feel it slip through your fingers." Because by then I, María Dorotea del Carmen, was already gone, under the ground. Patricio walked with the bucket hanging from his arm, shifting his weight from one side of his body to the other, parting the mist and his nostalgia until he reached the well. "But be careful, because trapped water is bad water. It organizes itself. It'll rot you if you don't let it run." It was when he lifted the heavy wooden plank that a strange web rose up to meet him. That's how he described it later: a web that pulled him down. It was made of thread like spider-silk, and white in color. He fell into the water and began to drown. The web blinded him, held him under. He kicked, flailed his arms, couldn't come up, squeezed his eyes to hold in the pale light that still reached him, protecting a sense of up above, north, clouds, morning, afternoon, and night, and then everything again: the stars observing the knots on the tips of the leaves, those little arms the trees use for reaching out and caressing each other, the wind's path through the woods, the satisfied plants, orienting their bodies toward oxygen. Then he heard it. Vaguely at first, like a voice splayed out across several walls. Then louder, hammering at his hearing, driving deeper than his eardrum. Hence he would later say that he'd been lifted up. That a strange voice helped him rise again, floating, and scale the walls of the well without any rope or stairs: "Someday you'll know what happens when the world becomes a barricaded flood, someday whatever you've got inside you will be able to echo outward and throw itself around your words like a circle, just as water keeps its will intact between cycles: forward, forward, forward. Remember this like a secret at the foot of the tree that opens and gathers what you feel. This is your influence. Your little flush of ripe fruit. One day you'll speak with us again and you'll be here whenever you think, whenever you see your father helping you catch your breath, holding you in his arms, and asking God to protect you, to be together a little while longer. Meanwhile, push hard to fling the water out and see how it sinks, how it skirts the sunlight and twists away, tricking thirsty stalks and birds. That water will bear your eyes like a thorn in your flesh, an ache in the shoulders that swells in the night. Take in the air and use it, take care of your voice that's with me always, above everything, below everything.

"Cata! Oh god, Catita, please!" He shook her hard. She didn't wake up.

The fire lit the sky at different intervals. It grasped the roots of the trees, distributed its heat underground. The night flaunted its life jacket. Stripped to his underwear, hair wild, his sister in his arms, he crossed to the other side of the fence. His cheeks streamed with mournful water. The loose plank swung as they headed for the highway. They emerged onto the shoulder. The headlamps of the passing cars caught them in fragments, fleeting as a glance in the mirror. Patricio yelled, begged their rivers of light for help. He stuck out his thumb, but no one was taking them anywhere.

Can you hear it now? The world hums here and you have to be part of it. Water follows its course. A slow rain falls, the forests drink, they breathe, dream, burn."

ABOUT THE AUTHOR

SIMÓN LÓPEZ TRUJILLO is a Chilean writer and translator, and author of the novel *El vasto territorio* (2021), the poetry chapbook *Maestranza* (2018), and the poem-object *Intemperie* (2017). He has been awarded the Roberto Bolaño Award and has received grants and fellowships from the Chilean Ministry of Arts & Culture, the Pablo Neruda Foundation, and MacDowell.

ROBIN MYERS is a poet and translator. A 2025 National Book Award Finalist and 2023 National Endowment for the Arts Translation Fellow, her recent translations include *We Are Green and Trembling* by Gabriela Cabezón Cámara; *Death Takes Me* by Cristina Rivera Garza (co-translated with Sarah Booker); and *Bariloche, Love Training*, and *A Father Is Born* by Andrés Neuman, among many other works of poetry and prose.